JUDGE RANDALL
AND THE LECHMERE BUS

JUDGE RANDALL
AND THE LECHMERE BUS

TONY ROGERS

A Judge Randall Mystery

Other titles in the Judge Randall series:

ISBN: 978-1-7356835-8-4 (Paperback)
ISBN: 978-1-7356835-9-1 (Ebook)

Published by Quinn Cove Books

Many thanks to Joan Seymour for her editorial help.

Cover Design by Berge Design

To Carmela, Madeline, Victoria, Anna, Sonny and Owen

1

Judge Randall's handy if infrequent bus, the #69 to Lechmere, swooped to a stop where Jim's quiet side street met busy Cambridge Street. Until his retirement from the Massachusetts Superior Court four years earlier, Judge Jim Randall would not have combined the words 'swooped' and 'bus' even in his private thoughts, but now that his imagination and vocabulary were unleashed by being off the bench, he felt entitled to use whatever words he wanted. And the darn bus did in fact swoop; the stop at Jim's corner was the second after Harvard Square and the bus seemed impatient to get to the real world of East Cambridge and Beauty Shop Row. Hence it didn't slow to a stop, it *swooped* to a stop.

"Morning," Jim muttered to the bus driver, a middle-aged black man with blunt features and a gruff manner coupled with the hidden kindness of the gruff. Jim didn't know the driver's name, but his number was 23853; Jim knew that from hearing repeated announcements over the loudspeaker: "Bus being driven by driver number 23853." Jim took the bus less frequently now that he was no longer a judge, but when he had commuted to the courthouse, he was a regular.

The bus not only swooped, it kneeled, genuflected, curtsied, and dipped to help passengers with mobility problems get on or off. The morning of the murder, it had dipped as far as it could at the stop in front of Rosie's

House of Beauty to let a wheelchair passenger on. While the passenger wheeled himself aboard, the driver put the bus in park, walked to the space reserved for people in wheelchairs, and locked the seat in the upright position. He didn't smile at the passenger (just doing my job, Jim imagined him saying) but he had a precise, proud way of lifting and locking the seat that made Jim smile. The driver returned to his seat and was about to raise the front end of the bus, when the gunman flashed through the door and fired two bullets into the driver's brain.

*

"What happened next?" Assistant District Attorney Ted Conover asked Jim. The two of them had known each other for twenty years, almost as long as Jim had been a judge. Jim had been on the bench for less than a year when Ted tried his first case in Jim's courtroom, the robbery of an East Cambridge jewelry store. He had done a good job for a brand-new prosecutor, Jim remembered. A little nervous as was to be expected, but with solid litigating skills. In the twenty years since, Ted had prosecuted countless cases in Jim's courtroom and Jim considered him a friend. Ted remained an Assistant DA, never aspiring to the top position, but as the longest serving and one of the most respected ADA's, he essentially ran the District Attorney's office.

"Jim, pay attention, what happened next?"

Jim shook himself back to Ted's question. "What happened next was pandemonium, shouting, unmitigated panic. The passengers struggled to exit the bus, blocking the aisles. Screaming in a way I had never heard before, flat out panic. The gunman had fled out the door so the danger was past, but the panic inside the bus grew. Someone with more presence of mind than me called the police, and you know the rest."

"Two shots, you say? Both aimed at the bus driver's head?"

"Correct. Two shots in quick succession, fired at close range."

"Describe the gunman."

"Young white male, 5'9" or 5'10", wearing a dark warmup jacket, black knit cap and wraparound sunglasses. I only got a glimpse, but he looked more like a spoiled rich kid playing gun-toting thug than an honest-to-god hit man."

Ted looked amused. "Judge Randall, always sticking to the facts."

"Now that I am off the bench, I am free to embellish at will, and don't you make fun of me."

"Never, I envy your freedom. The killing sounds to me like revenge, or a thrill killing, or maybe a gang initiation. Take your pick. We've got security camera footage, multiple eyewitnesses, and two spent bullets. I don't think it will take long to locate the killer."

Jim walked home from Ted's office. The walk was two miles and he had often walked it when he worked in the courthouse, but he walked it now because he couldn't bring himself to get back on a #69 bus. Eventually, but not yet, not now.

Cambridge Street between Inman and Kendall squares is a little United Nations: a Caribbean grocery store, Portuguese and Brazilian restaurants, a bar for the college crowd featuring indie bands, a live poultry store, and more beauty shops per square block than Jim had ever imagined, let alone seen, hence Beauty Shop Row. Since Jim had christened it thus, he walked it now as if he owned it.

"Hello?" he answered his phone as he walked.

"Jim, it's Ted. The bus driver's name was Ricardo Abbé. Naturalized citizen, born in Haiti, emigrated in 1994. Wife, two grown kids. Drove for the MBTA for twenty-two years."

"Criminal record?"

"None. Not even a traffic ticket."

"I frequently ride the #69 bus. I saw Mr. Abbé many times, although I never spoke to him. He looked unfriendly, but he took pride in his job. This morning, just before he was shot, I noted how sensitively he accommodated a wheelchair passenger. Who would want to kill a man like that?"

"That's what we want to know. Think you could pick the shooter out of a lineup when we catch him?"

"I doubt it. I only got a glimpse, and his face was hidden by a knit cap and sunglasses."

"But you are known for your powers of observation."

"Not on the Lechmere bus. I ride it so often, I zone out when I'm on it."

Jim lived in a townhouse equidistant between Harvard Square and Inman Square. Half-a-house Jim called it (or a halfway house, when he was in a sardonic mood) since it was one of two townhouses carved out of what once had been a large single-family home. The townhouse had lots of stairs, which so far, nearing the age of seventy, Jim could still climb; he wasn't sure what he would do when he couldn't, move into Pat's Beacon Hill apartment? Patricia Knowles, former fellow judge on the Superior Court and after both of them had retired, his significant other. Her apartment had less square footage than Jim's townhouse, but it was all on one floor. He spent many nights there, and she at Jim's, but they were content to have occasional solo nights.

"Your place tonight?" Pat said over the phone.

"Good. I'm feeling a little shaky."

"Who can blame you?"

"It all happened so fast. The driver had just returned to his seat after helping a wheelchair passenger when the gunman appeared out of nowhere and fired. Bam! Bam! Two shots, straight to the head! Pat, it was awful."

"I can't imagine. We can talk it out when I get there."

"Pick up something to eat, will you?"

"Or we could go out. Someplace familiar. Duck, Duck, Goose, perhaps?"

"Not tonight. Solitude and you are what I need tonight."

"Be right over."

They didn't talk about the shooting at first, not until dinner. And when they did, they eased into the subject. Both had presided over many murder trials as judges, but neither had witnessed a murder. "Every judge should witness a murder before they try a murder case," Jim said.

"The chances of witnessing a murder are slim. You would need volunteer victims."

"You're always so practical."

Pat reached across the table and gripped Jim's hand. "Are you going to be able to sleep tonight?"

"I don't know."

"Will you investigate the shooting?"

"Probably not. Ted thinks they won't have much trouble solving this one. The bus had security cameras, and there are plenty of eyewitnesses."

"Good, I don't want you to get involved. You need distance to be a good sleuth, and you lack it in this case."

Easy for Pat to say. He knew she was right but he couldn't stop replaying the murder in his mind – the shooter leaping onto the bus, shooting, disappearing. Each time Jim remembered it a little differently – the shooter: 5'8" or a giant? A teen or older? Growing older with each replay. Over and over, driving Jim nuts.

He awoke exhausted. It was light outside.

He was alone in bed. He got up and found Pat in the kitchen reading the paper.

"How long have you been up?" he asked.

"Not long."

"What time is it?" Jim glanced at the wall clock, which was always a few minutes fast. He had needed a new clock for months. 8:18 according to the clock, which meant it was 8:15.

"I didn't fall asleep until recently."

"No, you slept. Not immediately, but eventually."

"How could you tell? Were you awake?"

"I can tell by your breathing."

Jim went to the counter and poured himself a cup of coffee. With his back to Pat, he said, "One of the things I worried about in my sleep is how can I learn more about the bus driver, which made me think of Sasha."

"You said you weren't going to get involved."

"And you believed me?"

"Not for a second, but I like to keep my options open. Once in a while you surprise me."

*

Sasha Cohen was a reporter for the Boston *Globe*. Jim had met her when she was a reporter for an alternative weekly which had since gone out of business. Jim was very fond of her. She was enterprising, dogged, not easily dissuaded; serious, perhaps to a fault, but able to take a joke and occasionally tell one. They met as usual at The Long Gone coffeehouse in Inman Square, Jim's hangout of choice, and in retirement, his *de facto* chambers.

"When you texted me this morning about the shooting of the bus driver, did you know that I'm covering the story for the *Globe*?" Sasha said.

"No, but I'm not surprised. You're the best reporter the *Globe* has. What have you learned so far?"

"Ricardo Abbé was an exemplary employee. 15 years with the MBTA, good attendance, spotless driving record. He and his widow, Misha, lived on East Canton Street in East Cambridge. His widow is too distraught to talk."

East Canton Street was one of the many side streets off Beauty Shop Row. Jim liked the side streets but knew them mainly from glimpsing them from the Lechmere bus or while walking between the courthouse and home.

"The police are perfectly capable of handling this case, but I'm involved whether I like it or not. I rode the Lechmere bus to the courthouse many, many times when I was a judge, and never saw a murder on it until now. It feels personal."

"Of course, Jim."

"We'll keep each other informed, right?"

Sasha smiled. "Of course we will."

"Why are you smiling?"

"For no reason."

"Because if you're making fun of me, don't."

"Never. I would never make fun of such an august personality."

"Good, because you don't want to get on Judge Randall's bad side."

"There! *You* smiled."

"I did not."

"A sliver of a smile, I saw it. Quite cute, in fact."

"That does it. I am not cute and how dare you say so."

Sasha lowered her head in an attempt to hide her amusement. "Sorry, Jim, I mean Judge Randall. You are not at all cute. Quite plain in fact."

"Now wait a minute!"

Sasha was already leaving. "Bye, Jim."

Jim walked home from The Long Gone in a better mood. Two reasons: he liked Sasha, and he was glad to be involved in a case again. After retirement he had grown increasingly bored until he appeared on a panel at the

Harvard Divinity School with an MIT professor and a controversial evangelical preacher, a preacher who was found dead behind the school in the morning. Thus began Jim's second career as an amateur detective and the end of his boredom.

As Jim approached his street, he saw students streaming out of the high school and flooding the sidewalk. A fire alarm had been pulled, apparently. Was it a drill, a prank, or for real? Jim reached his house half a block away and unlocked his front door, taking a last look at the students streaming out of the school.

An email from Ted Conover was waiting for him. Jim read it in his kitchen.

"An arrest has been made in the Abbé murder. Meet me after work at the usual place and I'll fill you in."

Ted's usual place was the Ipsa Loquitur, a lawyers' bar near the courthouse, which Jim had avoided while he was a judge, too many courthouse lawyers. but in retirement it had become his usual place to have a drink with Ted.

Jim thought of Ipsa Loquitur as a smoky bar sans smoke. Instead of smoke, the air was thick with courthouse gossip. Jim and Ted sat on stools at the end of the bar.

"Young fellow, mid-20's, 5'8", done juvenile time for assault and battery, now washes dishes at the Chow and Stars. What? Why the skeptical look?" Ted asked.

"The shooter I saw was in his teens."

"Are you sure? You didn't sound sure of his age before."

"I've had time to think about it."

"As opposed to second-guessing yourself?"

"Maybe."

"Will you come to a lineup?"

"Yes."

Ted signaled for another beer. "You want another?" he asked Jim, who was drinking red wine, no surprises there.

"No, I don't think so. I'm joining Pat for dinner."

Ted looked around the bar at lawyers making merry, a sorry sight. "I'm going to miss this place."

"Are you going somewhere?"

"Not now, but I'm beginning to think about life after the law."

"The DA's office would grind to a halt if you weren't there."

"Not true. That's what I felt about you and the court but look, you left, and the court is doing better than ever."

Jim checked Ted's face to see if he was joking. His voice rarely varied from courtroom serious, but his face had trouble suppressing smiles. "That's not what I heard. I heard the court barely functions without me," Jim countered.

Ted chuckled. "I'll let you know when the lineup will be." He slid off his stool.

"Hey, what about the tab?"

Ted waved bye–bye over his shoulder. "Sorry, gotta run."

2

The lineup was held the next morning in the basement of the courthouse, near the holding cells. The men in the cells had slept on the floor or on benches that folded down from the wall. Some looked as if they had paced the floor all night. The odor in the corridor mixed stale urine with fresh panic. The men who were awake checked Jim out as he walked by. None gave any sign of recognizing him.

Jim was taken to a viewing room at the end of the corridor. A young women Jim recognized from the DA's office nodded to him. "Good morning, Judge. Are you ready?"

"I am."

She triggered the intercom. "Bring them in."

Six men, numbered by signs, lined up, looking bored, pissed, incredulous – none looked guilty, but in Jim's experience, the guilty rarely did.

"Take your time, Judge."

"Thanks. I know the drill."

Jim studied the men. He knew in an instant that none of the men was the man with the gun who jumped onto the bus and shot the driver twice in the head. Not even close.

But he studied the men one by one to make sure – too tall, too short, too old, too bored.

Jim turned to the woman from the DA's office and shook his head.

"Are you sure?"

"Absolutely."

"Thank you, Judge. We'll let you know what develops."

Jim left the courthouse and started for home. He got as far as Sciarappa Street before he changed his mind and waited for a bus. The #69. He had to get on the #69 again if he had a hope of being objective. Toss your qualms aside, Jim, be a mensch.

Once he climbed aboard and swiped his Charlie Card, it felt as normal as everyday, not dangerous in any way.

He took a seat in the first row past the rear exit; as he did, the emotions of the shooting flooded over him and he almost bolted from the bus. But it was too late, the doors had closed. Fortunately, because he felt a special duty to solve this case. As good as Ted's staff and the local police were, Jim had the unique advantage of having witnessed the crime. How many amateur detectives can say that about a case? So he needed to absorb everything he could about the bus and its riders, not just today but every day; not because he expected to see the young shooter jump on the bus again, but to study the regular riders for clues.

The riders were mostly workers going to and from offices, hospitals, restaurants, and shops. Jim had watched them on many occasions but never for any reason other than people watching. How strange to look at the riders now from a detective's point of view, how strange, as if he had never ridden the bus before. There was the sleepy man who kept nodding off, the jumpy man who couldn't sit still, the woman with a baby who kept checking her watch. There was a woman with swollen ankles, a man wearing paint-spattered clothing, a young man absorbed in his phone.

The bus passed East Canton Street. On the spur of the moment, Jim pushed the stop-requested button. The bus swooped to a stop.

Jim debussed (if airline passengers can deplane, why can't bus passengers debus?). The door shut behind him, and Jim set off down East Canton Street.

The houses were tidy, multi-family wood frame houses. Jim was struck by the stillness on the street even though busy Cambridge Street abutted one end and an auto body shop, a moving company, and a Target abutted the other. He didn't know in which house Ricardo Abbé had lived (and presumably his widow still did), but it didn't matter for Jim's present purposes. What was the mood, the tone of the street? An oasis from the bustle of the city. There were sprawling housing projects on nearby streets, but small-scale East Canton Street retained a personal feel.

Why would anyone who lived on this street be a target for a gunman?

Maybe Abbé hadn't been a target, maybe he was the unlucky victim of someone who wanted a kill under his belt. Or maybe it was a case of mistaken identity. A botched gang hit, maybe? There was nothing to suggest that Ricardo Abbé had anything to do with gangs, but it was possible.

Jim returned to Cambridge Street to wait for a bus. For some reason, he felt unusually dispirited – was this just another senseless killing in the land of senseless killings?

Jim stayed at Pat's that night. Beacon Hill was New Money perched on Old Boston, the antithesis of the immigrant communities of East Cambridge. Jim thought Beacon Hill a touch too self-satisfied but beautiful nonetheless. He climbed the hill to Pat's apartment thinking as he gasped for air that the climb might do him in someday. "Why did you two break up, you seemed so will suited?" "Well, it was like this, Your Honor, too steep a climb."

He had a key to her apartment, but Pat heard him coming and opened the door before he could.

"Hi."

"You're out of breath."

"I'm old." He pecked her cheek. "But I'm gorgeous."

"Come in. I opened some wine, taking a chance you'd like red."

"Good guess."

"Languedoc-Roussillon."

"Music to my ears."

He sat down in her well-curated living room. Her easy chair seemed made for him. He emitted a sigh and stretched his legs full length. All was right in his world, except for the killing of a driver on the Lechmere bus.

Jim slept badly and next morning, momentarily, couldn't remember where he was. "Does that ever happen to you?" he asked Pat at the breakfast table.

"All the time."

"Really?"

"I exaggerate, but it definitely happens."

"Well, it never happened to me on the bench. Occasionally my mind wandered, but I never forgot where I was," Jim said.

"Number one, work is a different category of existence, and number two, you sleep in two places, but you worked in only one courthouse. Problem solved."

"What would I do without you? Oh, I know."

"You know what you would do without me?"

"No, I was changing the subject. I know what I'm going to do this morning."

"I'm afraid to ask."

"I am going to talk to a bus driver or two. Want to join me?"

"No, thank you. You're on your own."

When breakfast was done, Jim walked across the river to the Lechmere bus station. The station was in sorry shape, a shack by any other name. It was to be replaced in a year or two as part of the redevelopment of the area, but for now it was an embarrassment. Buses idled there at the end of their run before they headed back to Harvard Square. Jim approached one driver sitting on the steps of his bus, eating a sandwich.

"Hi, got a minute?"

"A minute, then I'm off to Harvard Square."

"I'll make it quick. I'm Judge Randall, formerly of the Massachusetts Superior Court. I was on the bus when your colleague, Ricardo Abbé, was shot and killed. Did you know him?"

The driver wiped his mouth and stood. "You saw it happen?"

"I did."

The bus driver shook his head. "Must have been horrible. Nobody who knew Ricardo can understand it. He was a good guy. Who would want to kill him?"

"That's what I'm trying to find out. What's the word among his fellow drivers?"

"Nobody has a clue. He was a good family man. We used to give him trouble for being so boring. 'Your wife's going to leave you for somebody more exciting,' we'd say. He'd say, 'I'm so good in bed, she'll never leave me.' He was okay, he could give as well as he could take."

"I rode his bus many times. He struck me as gruff on the surface, kind underneath."

The driver thought for a minute. "Yeah, I guess that's fair. I've been trying to remember if I ever heard other drivers say an angry word about Ricardo – did he piss somebody off? Did he have enemies? But I can't remember anything like that. He came to work, he did his job, he went home. Like I say, a good guy."

"Thanks. You've been very helpful. What's your name?"

"Jerome. Gotta get back in the saddle."

"Can I ride with you?"

"You going to Harvard Square?"

"Yep. I live near the high school."

"Then jump on board, but don't expect a free ride just because we talked." Jerome had dark brown eyes, light brown skin, and a tired face. Jim guessed he was in his late thirties. He hadn't smiled until he warned Jim not to expect a free ride, at which point his entire face burst into a smile.

Jim followed him onto the bus. "Don't worry, my Charlie Card has more than enough to cover my fare."

Jerome started the bus. The motor coughed a few times, then began running with authority. Jim sat on the bench-like seat nearest the front door. The wheelchair seat which Ricardo Abbé had lifted and locked with such care before he was shot was immediately to Jim's left. The memory made Jim shudder.

At the Cambridge Hospital stop, several passengers wearing hospital scrubs exited and an elderly man with a walker got on. Jim offered him his seat and stood by the front door waiting for his stop.

"Thanks for your help," he said to Jerome the driver as he got off the bus.

Jerome nodded. "Catch the bastard, okay?"

Jim stepped off the bus into a swarm of high school students on their lunch break, heading most likely to the pizza parlor up the block. He liked living in an area with lots of students but could do without them when they were swarming. They moved as one and parted for no one.

Every weekday morning, the Lechmere-Harvard Square bus carried scores of students going to school. Every morning, if Jim was walking past the bus stop when the students disembarked, he had to be careful not to get swallowed by the crowd.

He headed down the street to the pizza parlor. A seriously long line of students stood at the counter waiting to order. Jim approached the line. He raised his voice.

"I'm a retired judge of the Massachusetts Superior Court looking into the shooting of the driver of the #69 bus. Do any of you ride that bus?"

The students were unsure whether to answer. They looked at each other questioningly.

Jim added, "None of you will get in trouble. I'm investigating this case on my own. I was on the bus when it happened."

A girl said, "You saw the shooting?"

"I did."

"Was it horrible?"

"Very. It haunts me still. Did any of you know the driver, Ricardo Abbé?"

Another girl said, "He was a kind man. I liked him."

"I'd like to talk to you and anyone else who knew him, but I'm holding up the line. I'll sit at that table in the corner and hope some of you will join me."

Jim nodded an apology to the owner and sat down at the corner table. Jim usually didn't do things like this, as a judge he didn't have to. He felt self-conscious now. Then a student approached.

"Sit down. Please," Jim said.

Then another and another.

"Thanks for coming. Anything you can tell me."

A girl said, "We just want to tell you that none of us saw Mr. Abbé do anything that might have led to this. He was a gentle man. He looked fierce but he was gentle."

"Yeah," a young man echoed, "never an angry word. Some drivers give us a hard time. I don't blame them, students can act like jerks, but Ricardo never did."

Jim nodded. "A lot of students ride the #69. I live a block away and see them every day. Is it possible that Mr. Abbé did or said something in the past that a passenger took personally, maybe too personally?"

"Was that Ricardo's last name? Abbé?"

"Yes. Originally from Haiti."

"We knew he was Haitian, we could tell by his accent, we just didn't know his last name. Who shot him?"

"A young man, probably in his late teens," Jim replied.

"No one from the school. If it were a kid from the school, someone would know."

"We sent flowers to Mr. Abbé's widow," a young woman added.

Jim said, "A nice gesture. How did you know where she lives?"

"A kid in my class lives on her street."

"Think he'd talk to me?"

"He's shy," the girl who spoke first said. "He might talk to you if I asked."

"Would you?"

"You promise he won't get in any trouble?"

"I absolutely promise. What's his name?"

"Marcus Jackson. I'll ask him."

"Tell Marcus I'll wait for him here after school today."

"Our last class ends at 3:20."

"I'll be here. Tell him I'll understand if he doesn't want to talk."

Marcus Jackson was a tall, young African American, who hunched his shoulders as if embarrassed by his height. At 3:25 he warily approached Jim's table. "Judge Randall?"

"Yes. Sit down please. You must be Marcus Jackson."

"Yes, sir." Marcus sat down. "I don't know what you want, but I'm here."

"And I appreciate that. I'm investigating the shooting of Ricardo Abbé. I'm doing this on my own, I no longer have an official role, but I feel a personal obligation to identify the killer since I saw the shooting."

Marcus had a soft voice and an expression that was part-curiosity, part-get-off-my-back. "That's what I was told. You saw it?"

"I did."

"The shooter was white?"

"Correct."

"Good."

"Why do you say good?"

"Because whenever there's a shooting in Cambridge, people assume the shooter was a black kid. I'm tired of it. Sorry. No offense."

"None taken. I was told you live on East Canton Street."

Marcus nodded. "Two houses away from the Abbé's."

"Do you know Mrs. Abbé?"

"Not well. I say hello to her when I see her, that sort of thing."

"Have you seen her since the shooting?"

"No. My mom took some food over to her, but I haven't seen her."

"I've got a question for you. Think it over before you answer. It's a lot to ask." Jim paused to let his words sink in. "Okay?"

"What's your question?"

"Would you or your mother be willing to carry a message to Mrs. Abbé?"

"What do you mean?"

"If I write down my phone number and email address for Mrs. Abbé, would you or your mother take it to her? I'd like to talk to her."

Marcus seemed unsure. "I'd have to ask Mom."

"Talk it over. I don't want to involve either of you against your will."

Another pause. "Okay," Marcus said. "I'll talk to Mom."

Jim scribbled his contact information on a page in his pocket notebook, tore the page from the notebook, and handed the page to Marcus. "Here. My phone number and email. No hard feelings if you or your mother want no part of this."

Marcus's text came the next morning. "Mom wants to meet with you before she agrees to anything. I'll come too."

Jim's reply. "Tell me where and when and I'll be there."

Jim, Marcus, and Mrs. Jackson met at a convenience store close to East Canton Street. Three pots of brewed coffee and four tall stools made a window counter into a miniature Long Gone. Mrs. Jackson's first name was Lanelle, Jim learned when Marcus introduced her.

"Pleased to meet you, Mrs. Jackson," Jim responded.

"Marcus said you were a judge," Lanelle Jackson said. She looked too young to be the mother of a teenager. Marcus seemed quietly proud of her, but Jim acknowledged that could be a figment of his imagination.

"I was. Twenty-one years on the Superior Court. When I retired, I stumbled into investigating crime. The death of Ricardo Abbé feels personal to me since I saw it happen."

Lanelle Jackson nodded. "That's what Marcus told me, and you want me or him to deliver a note to his widow."

"Yes. I would like to talk to her but I know she's going through hell, so I want to give her space to refuse."

Lanelle had the face of a women predisposed to see the good in people but who had learned the hard way that people could disappoint. "Mrs. Abbé's hurting real bad. I don't want to make things worse for her."

"Neither do I. If she doesn't want to talk to me, I'll understand. But I hope that by learning more about her husband, I'll get a better idea of who did this to him. I will tread lightly, I promise. Her husband struck me as a man of dignity. I was impressed with how he went about his job. We can meet anywhere she wants."

"Write out your message and I'll give it to her."

3

Jim didn't hear anything for a week and began to assume he never would. He wasn't sure if Lanelle Jackson had decided not to deliver Jim's note, or if the widow Abbé wanted no part of what Jim was requesting. Then, a phone call.

"Is this Judge Randall?"

"Yes."

"This is Misha Abbé. You wanted to talk to me?" Her voice was firm but full of grief.

"Yes. Thank you for calling. I rode your husband's bus many times, and I was on his bus the day he died."

Silence for a moment. "Your note said you were trying to find Ricardo's killer. Is that true?"

"Yes."

"And that you used to be a judge."

"I was."

"I'll give you a few minutes of time. Come to my apartment tomorrow afternoon at 3. Do you know where I live?"

"On East Canton Street, but what number?"

"35."

35 East Canton Street was two blocks from Cambridge Street. A three-story stucco house with a wooden front porch. Misha Abbé lived on the second floor. Jim rang the doorbell.

The door opened a crack and a sad black face peered out.

"Mrs. Abbé? I'm Judge Randall."

The door swung open. Mrs. Abbé was a woman in her fifties. She had the saddest eyes Jim had ever seen. "Come in." She led Jim into the living room.

"Sit down," she gestured to a patterned sofa. "I miss my husband so much."

"I hope I'm not making things worse for you."

"I invited you here. If you can help find Ricardo's killer, I'll be eternally grateful. Can I get you coffee?"

"No, I'm fine, thanks."

She sat. "What do you want to know?"

"Did your husband have enemies?"

"No. He scared some people because he looked fierce, but he wasn't fierce at all. The only people who didn't like Ricardo were people who didn't know him."

"He didn't have any longstanding quarrels with anybody at work?"

"No, and I'm sure of that. He brought his worries home, and he never expressed anything about quarrels at work."

"What did he do before he became a bus driver?"

"He was a bus driver for twenty-two years, so that was a long time ago."

"I realize, but what did he do before?"

"He tried to start his own lawn care company, mowing, snow shoveling, that sort of thing. He couldn't make a go of it, hard to get help, not enough customers, so he chose something steadier. Driving for the MBTA."

"Did anything happen during those years that looks relevant in hindsight?"

"A few years ago he turned a fellow driver in for skimming the till. Ricardo got in trouble at first because the driver had a union rep on his side, but eventually the driver fled town and the union rep was exposed for being in on the take."

"Tell me more about that."

"Nothing more to tell. The union rep went to jail and the driver who fled was never found. Ricardo received a commendation for exposing the scheme."

"Your husband sounds like a good man."

Tears came to Mrs. Abbé's eyes. "The best."

"I'm sorry," Jim said. "I'll leave."

"No. Please continue. I want to find Ricardo's killer."

"He never received threats for turning in the driver?"

"He did, but as soon as the driver fled town and the union rep went to prison, the threats stopped." Mrs. Abbé stood. "Are you sure you don't want coffee?"

"Actually, now I do. Thanks."

Jim looked around the tidy apartment while she was gone. A patterned sofa. A leather chair, cracked and faded, the imprint of Ricardo Abbé's sizeable body still visible. A bookcase beside the chair. A reading lamp still on – Ricardo would be right back.

Mrs. Abbé emerged from the kitchen, startling Jim. She handed him his coffee.

"Thanks. I won't keep you much longer, and I appreciate the time you've given me."

"I welcome the company. Our son and daughter came for the funeral but had to go back to work, and the house seems so empty."

"What kind of work do they do?"

"Stan is an orthopedist at New York-Presbyterian Hospital. Moesha runs a charter school."

"In Boston?"

"No. Hartford. Her husband teaches at Trinity College."

"You must be proud of them."

"At the moment it's hard to feel proud about anything."

"Yes. Of course."

"Judge Randall, did you hear Ricardo say anything after he got shot?"

"I'm sorry, I didn't. There was panic, a rush to get off the bus before there was more shooting. If your husband spoke, I didn't hear it in the mayhem."

"Did he suffer?"

"I don't think he even knew what happened. The medical examiner said death was instantaneous."

Mrs. Abbé nodded. "Thank God for that."

Jim didn't stay much longer. He thanked Mrs. Abbé and promised to tell her if he learned anything of note. At her apartment door, she gripped his hands in hers, her eyes a little less sad. He thought he detected gratitude in her eyes, as if she had been speaking to her dead husband through him.

The thought unnerved him. Neither as judge nor as amateur detective had he played that role and he didn't feel prepared. But as he walked Cambridge Street after he left her apartment, he told himself that he had done okay and may have done some good. Suck it up, big guy.

He pulled out his phone and called Ted.

When Ted answered, Jim heard traffic noise in the background.

"It's Jim. I'm walking towards your office."

"So am I. I just pleaded a case at the courthouse. Do you want to see me?"

"I do. I just spoke with Mrs. Abbé, the widow of the murdered bus driver. If you've got five minutes, I'll fill you in."

"Meet me in the coffee shop next door to my office."

Ted beat Jim to it. He smiled when he saw Jim, "Sit. Talk. But be brief, I've got a meeting in five minutes. What did you learn from the widow?"

"When we started talking, she looked like someone whose soul has been crushed. She clearly has no idea of who could have killed her husband, but she did tell me that her husband had turned in another bus driver who was skimming the till, and that the driver had fled and remained in hiding to this day. A union rep served time for the scheme. I didn't learn the names of either."

"I can easily get the names. I would imagine the till-skimming driver would hold a grudge against Abbé for turning him in, wouldn't you?"

"I imagine he would, yes."

"Thanks, Jim. This is helpful."

"I expect formal praise and adulation when the killer is caught."

"Don't hold your breath. I've got to go." Ted patted Jim's shoulder as he left.

Jim slowly drank his coffee. He wasn't going to be rushed. This was a takeout coffee shop for lawyers in a hurry, not The Long Gone, he knew that, but Judge Randall was not to be rushed. Judge Randall had his own time zone (Randall Standard Time – RST). He sat until he had proved his point, then walked the few blocks to Beauty Shop Row, where he caught a #69 home.

*

Jim and Pat ate at Duck, Duck, Goose that night. Bruce, at the front desk, welcomed them warmly. "Welcome back. Where have you been?"

"Eating elsewhere."

"Don't blame you."

"I was kidding. You know we love it here."

Bruce seated them at their favorite table, in the front corner, by the windows.

"You don't let anyone else sit at this table when we're not here. Right?"

Bruce handed them their menus. "Of course not. Unthinkable. Enjoy your meal."

Pat skimmed the menu. "How did your meeting with the bus driver's widow go this morning?" she asked Jim as she skimmed.

They had not seen each other for a couple of days, which was unusual for them. They stayed together at his place or hers most nights, but skipping a night or two did not affect their relationship. They had lived alone long enough prior to becoming a couple to welcome occasional solitude.

"The widow Abbé broke my heart. Hemingway said that grace under pressure equals courage. Mrs. Abbé taught me that courage is dignity in grief. Her late husband had reported a fellow bus driver for theft several years ago, and the driver had fled to parts unknown. It doesn't take a leap of imagination to picture the driver plotting revenge against Ricardo Abbé for ruining his life."

"Do you believe that?"

"You sound skeptical."

"Well? Do you?"

"Not a chance. Too easy."

"Did the Abbé's have kids?"

"Yes. Two. Both accomplished professionals. Unlikely killers, if that's where your mind is going."

A young waiter they didn't recognize approached the table. "Would either of you like a drink before dinner?"

Jim answered, "I haven't looked at the wine list. Any new reds?'

"A Cab from the Salinas Valley."

Jim shook his head. "Not California. French or Italian. You had a Ventoux the last time we were here. Is it still on your list?"

"We took it off the list, but I believe we have a few bottles left. Would you like a bottle of that if we have it?"

"Okay, Pat?" Jim asked. She nodded in affirmation, if not enthusiasm.

"A bottle of that, please," Jim told the young waiter. When the young man had left, Jim remarked, "Am I wrong or does he look twelve?"

"You're wrong."

Their dinner was uneventful, a night together welcome. Jim was unusually tired and went straight to bed when they got home. Pat read in bed, but her reading lamp didn't keep Jim awake.

4

"Jim? Can you come to a lineup this morning?"

"Like the last one?"

"So that wasn't the best, but can you?" Ted sounded unfazed.

"Depends on the time."

"11 or thereabouts."

"I'll be there thereabouts."

He decided to walk. He left enough time to stop for coffee at The Long Gone. On the way he passed an apothecary, a doctor's office, a rehab hospital, and Cambridge City Hospital. Sirens could be heard throughout the day and much of the night as ambulances took patients to one of the facilities. A good neighborhood to get sick in, and if you reached The Long Gone without needing medical care, you could contemplate your mortality over a cup of coffee.

"Mornin', Judge. What can I get you this morning?" the barista asked.

"An answer to life's mysteries."

"Small, medium, or large?"

"Small. I have to identify a killer after I leave here."

"No kidding?" The barista pulled the lever for house blend. "Small house!" he announced much more loudly than he needed to given that Jim was standing directly in front of him. It was as if the coffee wouldn't be coffee if the barista didn't shout its name. Confucius said that correctly naming things was the first step to wisdom. Maybe the barista was a Confucian.

"Thanks." Jim took his coffee to a table in the middle.

He hoped the lineup would include the killer, and that he, Jim, could be the one to relay the good news to Mrs. Abbé.

Same depressing viewing room, different cast of characters, all wearing sunglasses and knit caps pulled low like the killer's.

A youngish man in the middle could be the one. Jim asked Ted to have the young man step forward.

Ted keyed the intercom. "Number 3, step forward please."

Jim studied the young man's face. Could be. The nose and chin looked as Jim remembered. The height and weight were similar. Age? Maybe not; number three looked older than the shooter.

Jim weighed his response.

"Take your time," Ted said.

Jim turned to Ted. "I'm not sure. Number 3 is a possibility. Wish I could be more definite."

"None of the others?"

"Nope. None of the others."

He felt dispirited when he left the courthouse. He had to find another way to spend his time in retirement, a way that didn't include crime. Mentoring teenagers, perhaps, but he lacked the patience. Become a younger boy's Big Brother, but he would probably scare the daylights out of young boys. Get a cup of coffee at The Long Gone, sit at a rear table, and brood. There's a plan.

He had barely sat with his coffee when Ernie Farrell texted him.

Social media loves the bus driver murder. Can't get enough. Want me to fill you in on what's being said?

What do you think?

Are you at The Long Gone?

How did you guess?

Stay there.

Ernie Farrell was indirectly responsible for Jim's post-retirement avocation. After a year of post-retirement boredom, Jim had agreed to represent him in court when Ernie was charged with vehicular homicide. It was Jim's first foray back into the courts after he left the bench, and his first ever as a defense attorney. Ernie – a young man in his twenties – made his living as a computer guru, and his tech smarts had often helped Jim in his investigations. Ernie's office was across the Cambridge/Somerville city line three blocks from Inman Square and The Long Gone.

Ernie was a compact man, all nervous energy, not a wasted inch. On the surface he looked nonchalant but a foot or a finger was always tapping, giving him away.

Whenever he debriefed Jim, he began without preamble, as if he were continuing a conversation that had been interrupted in mid-sentence. He started talking as he was sitting down.

"All the usual crazies are spinning theories. What is throwing them for a loop is that the shooter was white and the victim black. In white America, it's supposed to be the other way round. I forgot to get coffee." Ernie made that discovery when he reached for his coffee cup. "Be right back."

He returned a moment later with a steaming cup.

"What did you get?" Jim asked, not particularly caring but always glad to hear Ernie's responses.

"I'm not sure. I think it's Dominican."

"You were saying."

"What unnerves me is some of the stuff I'm reading on the dark web. Somehow the crazy and afraid have latched onto the fact that Ricardo Abbé was a dark-skinned immigrant to prove that white people are in mortal danger. Imagine. A dark-skinned immigrant is killed by a white guy, but it's white people who are in mortal danger. Their reasoning, if you can call it such, is that dark-skinned immigrants are taking over this country, and that killing them is justified self-defense. I know, I know, Abbé was not a threat to anybody, I'm just telling you what's popping up on nut-job sites."

Jim didn't reply.

"What are you thinking?" Ernie asked.

"When identity is lost, fury fills the void."

Ernie nodded. "Have you ever seen it this bad before?"

"Yes, the sixties. JFK, MLK, and RFK assassinated. Race riots. The Vietnam War."

"I'm glad I wasn't alive then."

"I don't blame you."

"Alive pre-computer I mean. I don't know how I would have earned a living. Speaking of which, I have to get back to my office."

"You haven't touched your coffee."

"So I haven't." He stood for a moment, perfectly still, then propelled himself out the door.

*

Jim spent most of the afternoon in his third-floor study, his favorite room. Floor-to-ceiling bookshelves, a leather chair with ottoman, a desk where he had spent many hours preparing for upcoming trials, and windows that looked out at more trees than one would expect in a densely populated city like Cambridge. Jim liked being indoors as long as he could see outside.

This morning he tried to find a narrative thread that could explain how and why an experienced bus driver with a spotless record would be shot in plain view of a bus full of passengers. No connecting thread had come to him so far; plenty of facts with little connection. To solve a case, facts were not enough; they were essential but insufficient unto themselves. Facts need a narrative thread to be understood, facts need connective tissue.

Jim's best guess was that someone who wanted Ricardo Abbé dead had put the young shooter up to it. But maybe the intended target was the driver of the #68 bus and the young shooter had shot the wrong man. Or perhaps the shooter was someone with a grudge against bus drivers in general, who jumped on a #69 because it stopped near his house, not because Ricardo Abbé was the driver.

He was about to head to The Long Gone when Ted called.

"We located the bus driver who Ricardo Abbé turned in for skimming the till. He's in a Kansas City jail. I don't know how long he's been locked up. The local DA is questioning him. I'll let you know what he learns."

"Thanks." When Jim got off the phone, he changed his mind. Instead of going to The Long Gone, he walked to the park in view of the high school and sat on a bench. The missing bus driver turns up in a Kansas City jail – what to make of that? How long had he been incarcerated? Had he hired a hit man to kill Ricardo Abbé in retaliation for Abbé squealing on him?

Crossing his legs, Jim declared himself inadequate compared to every other detective, fictional or real. They always seemed to think three or four steps ahead. Jim didn't know what to do when he got off the park bench.

His phone rang. Wrestling it out of his pocket always proved a struggle, but he finally had it in his hand. "Hello?"

A woman's voice. "Is this Judge Randall?"

"Yes, it is. Who is this?"

"Misha Abbé, Judge. I'm calling to find out if you have learned who killed my husband."

"Good morning, Mrs. Abbé. The bus driver who fled after your husband turned him in for theft has been located. He's in a Kansas City jail."

"Is that good news?"

"Too soon to tell. It wouldn't be easy to arrange a Massachusetts murder from a Kansas City jail cell, but it wouldn't be impossible. I'll know more when we hear from the Kansas City DA."

She paused before replying. He remembered her heartbreaking dignity. "How many murder trials did you preside over, Judge Randall?"

"Far too many. People kill for trivial reasons. A personal slight. An old grudge. The hardest cases to prove are the ones that make no sense. We may never know for sure why your husband died. I hope that's not the case, but I want you to be prepared. I promise I won't give up, if that's any comfort."

There was silence on the other end of the phone, then Jim realized Mrs. Abbé was crying.

Jim let her cry. "I'll get off, Mrs. Abbé. I'll be in touch. Goodbye for now."

For long moments after he got off the phone, Jim wasn't sure where he was, then he remembered he was sitting on a park branch in front of the high school. Students were streaming from the school. One of them was Marcus Jackson.

Marcus was laughing with the young woman walking beside him. They were playing bumper cars with each other's hips. Jim jumped off the bench.

"Marcus!"

Marcus stopped. He didn't look pleased to see who had called him. He leaned down and whispered to the young woman to go on ahead and waited for Jim to catch up.

"Hey," Marcus said grudgingly, as Jim approached.

"Got a second?"

"Not more than that."

"I want to thank you for your help. Because of it, I am in touch with Mrs. Abbé, in fact I just got off the phone with her."

"No problem," Marcus said, starting to leave.

"Before you go. Has anything happened on your street recently that strikes you as strange?"

"Like what?"

"Unusual activity around the Abbé house? People hanging out on your street you've never seen before?"

"I mind my own business."

"I'm sure you do, but have you noticed anything out of the ordinary?"

"No. Is that all?"

"Yes. You have my number. Please contact me if you notice anything suspicious. Will you do that for me?"

Marcus shrugged. "I make no promises. Hey, I've got to catch up with my girlfriend. You're getting in the way of young love."

*

Jim stayed at Pat's that night. He felt old, very old. The walk up Beacon Hill almost killed him. I've got to take better care of myself, he muttered to himself as he rang her bell. She had given him her key long ago, but he usually rang her bell to let her know he was coming.

She was knitting in the living room.

He hung his coat in the closet. "Since when did you take up knitting?"

"I took it up when we were colleagues on the court, but you didn't notice."

He sat on the sofa next to her. "Why did you keep it secret?"

"We weren't a couple then, there was a lot I didn't tell you."

"Really?"

"Little things of no significance, like my knitting. Anyway I gave it up. I only took it up again recently."

"Why?"

"Why did I start or why did I stop?"

"Both."

"No, you only get one question. Which will it be? Start or stop?"

"Your Honor, I can't take this pressure any longer. I want to go to jail."

They read in bed after dinner. She turned off her reading lamp before he did. "Good night."

"Night," he replied. Several minutes passed. "Pat?"

She already had fallen asleep. At the sound of his voice, she startled awake. "What? What is it?"

"Sorry to scare you. Nothing's wrong. I just want your opinion."

She struggled to a sitting position. "Opinion? About the murder?"

"About murder in general. What was the most ridiculous reason for murder among the cases you tried?"

"Can't it wait until morning?"

"But now that you're awake, what was the most ridiculous reason?"

"A husband killed his wife because she didn't keep an adequate supply of oatmeal on their kitchen shelves."

"I can understand that."

"You're not serious."

"Was he convicted?"

"Yes. Second degree murder. His lawyer argued that the motive proved insanity, but the jury didn't buy it. Why are you asking about this now?"

"None of the usual motives fit Ricardo Abbé's murder. If a drug deal or jealousy was involved, or a gambling debt hadn't been paid, why choose a crowded city bus to do the killing?"

Pat didn't reply. When Jim looked at her, he realized that she had fallen back to sleep. He rolled over and tried to turn his mind off so he could sleep.

Jim didn't hear from Ted for a few days. Then, a text: "Ipsa Loquitur, 6 pm today?"

When Jim walked into the Ipsa Loquitur, the buzz in the air had heft. Ted saw him and nodded. "You're late."

"You're early," Jim replied. Jim took the stool next to Ted.

"I've got two things to tell you, either one of which I could tell you over the phone but two seemed to warrant a face-to-face."

"Is that what having a drink after work is now called? A face-to-face? But we're sitting side-by-side."

Ted groaned. "Do you want to hear my news or not?"

"I'm just trying to lighten the mood. Go for it."

"The bus driver in a Kansas City jail had nothing to do with the murder, but we know who did." Ted looked annoyingly smug.

"Take them one at a time. Why are you sure the jailed bus driver had nothing to do with the murder?"

"He had been in solitary confinement for three weeks when the shooting occurred. Very limited means of communication with the outside world. Hard to arrange a hit."

"Okay, so he had nothing to do with it, no big surprise, but it does surprise me to hear you say you know who did the shooting."

"Yes. The young man from the second lineup. Six viewers picked him out of the lineup and you called him a possible. Further investigation convinced us he was our guy."

"I don't believe you."

"But it's true."

"I believe you mean what you say, but I don't believe he's the shooter. I thought more about it, and he doesn't match the shooter in looks or age."

"He's got a long record, a bogus alibi for the day of the murder, and by the way, he confessed."

"What did you offer him to get him to confess?"

"Second degree murder, which as you know carries the possibility of parole, unlike first degree. He doesn't want to die in prison."

"He'll recant. I've seen it before. A young man with a short rap sheet panics at the thought of a murder conviction and takes what he thinks is a good deal. Later, he rethinks his plea."

"Maybe, Jim, but for now the DA's office considers the case closed."

5

When Jim ate dinner alone in his kitchen, his mind wandered. Didn't matter if he was watching the PBS Newshour, didn't matter if he was reading the newspaper or a book, his mind wandered. Tonight he was eating prepared supermarket chicken which had no flavor, so his food didn't distract from his meanderings.

After twenty-one years on the bench when Jim had to hew closely to facts, he liked cutting his mind loose.

> *Which do I like better, being a detective or being a judge? Thank God I don't have to choose. Ted and his crew think they have the killer. Ted is a fair-minded man but he's human and once he makes up his mind, it's hard to get him to reconsider. Limbs That I Have Crawled Out On, by Jim Randall, available in hardcover and E book, paperback to follow.*

His food had turned cold while his mind wandered. It was dark outside; when did that happen? Given that he would turn seventy in less than a year, he owed it to life to pay attention to each and every remaining moment before he was no more. Noble thought, fat chance. Grumble, grumble, grumble.

The phone rang. He recognized Mrs. Abbé's number. "Good evening, Mrs. Abbé."

"Good evening, Judge. Do they know yet if the bus driver in a Kansas City jail is my Ricardo's killer?"

"He's not, Mrs. Abbé. The driver in question was in solitary confinement, cut off from the outside world, when your husband was killed. I'm sorry."

"What's going to happen now?" There was a touch of despair in her voice.

"Don't give up hope. Whoever did this will eventually be caught."

"Eventually?"

"I'm sorry, Mrs. Abbé, I know how frustrating it must be to wait."

"No, you don't, you can't possibly know."

"You're right, I can't possibly know."

"Someone hated my husband, Judge Randall. Someone hated him enough to kill him. God knows why, he was a good man, but that's the truth. Nothing besides hatred makes sense."

"You may be right, Mrs. Abbé."

Jim went upstairs soon after dinner. Pat was staying at her apartment that night. He missed her.

He turned on the bedroom TV, undressed and got into bed. He didn't feel at all sleepy but when he awoke in the morning, the TV was still on.

He shaved, showered, and walked to The Long Gone, his head at war with itself.

The Long Gone was extra busy this morning. Even the regulars seemed fidgety.

He texted Pat.

Good morning. I'm at The Long Gone. Can I come over when I leave here?

Her reply came a minute later.

By all means.

He felt calmer. It didn't take much. Three words from Pat were all it took.

Knowing that he had a safe haven to go to, he took his time finishing his coffee and corn muffin. He decided to walk to Pat's when he finished; the idea of taking the Lechmere bus still spooked him, plus the walk would improve his mood.

The sun was bright enough to take the edge off of the morning chill. His legs and lungs felt good. He walked swiftly past the hospitals and The Long Gone to the stretch of Cambridge Street that Jim called Beauty Shop Row. The number of storefronts devoted to beauty changed frequently, beauty being a fleeting thing; but for the moment, there were close to a dozen elbowing each other within half-a-dozen blocks. The first he came to touted eyebrow threading. Jim didn't know how one could thread an eyebrow let alone earn a living from it. The next shop advertised mani-pedi's, which he figured had to do with fingernails and toenails, the next shop waxing and facials. His favorite was Rosie's House Of Beauty, his favorite because of the glaring purple neon sign in its window. Subtly did not live on Beauty Shop Row, which is one reason it amused an uptight man like Jim.

He slowed in front of Rosie's to appreciate its garishness. Bad move on his part because a heavy-set woman with pink-tinted hair and a face of fury flew out the door and into Jim, almost toppling him. Fortunately his body had enough ballast to keep him upright. The woman was not the least bit contrite.

"Creep! You're blocking the sidewalk!"

Jim was dumbfounded but unhurt. "Madam, I think you are at fault."

A tall man with a big forehead and little hair appeared in the doorway through which the irate woman had just flown. He yelled at the woman. "And don't come back! You are no longer welcome here!"

The woman returned fire. "You think I would come back after the way you've treated me?"

The woman turned to Jim. "Can you imagine that? They butchered my hair, yet have the nerve to tell me not to come back. Can you believe that?"

"Madam, a moment ago you called me a creep, now I am your ally?"

She huffed, "Well, if you don't care when a woman is mistreated, go to hell." And she left loudly, a town crier of personal grievances.

The man in the doorway stepped out to see if Jim was okay. Jim assured him he was.

"The woman has a temper, that's for sure," the man said, shaking his head.

"Is she a regular?"

"Yeah, every few weeks. The staff dreads her visits."

The man went back inside, and Jim went on his way. The walk gave him a choice of two bridges on which to cross the Charles. He chose the Longfellow, longer to reach, nicer to cross. The view from the highest point of the bridge encompassed the wide river, looking more like a harbor here than a river. By the time he reached Beacon Hill, he had forgotten the bad-tempered woman.

*

The arraignment of the young man from the second lineup took place in the middle of the week. Jim made a point of being there. Seeing the suspect in court, watching him closely, convinced Jim more than ever that he was not the young man he had seen leap on the Lechmere bus and shoot Ricardo Abbé in the head. Jim stopped Ted in the hall when the morning's courtroom business was done.

"He's not the guy, Ted. You are making a mistake."

Ted grasped Jim's forearm, a friend, a warning, a back-off. "He confessed, Jim."

"Did he have counsel?"

"Didn't ask for one. He seemed eager to get it over with. The ADA who was at the arraignment said the kid seemed resigned to be convicted."

"Is he protecting someone?"

"If so, he's making a bad mistake."

"You told me he had served time in the past. True?"

"Yes. In a juvenile facility. Released when he was eighteen."

Jim shook his head. "Sounds like a beaten young man, worn down, no fight left. I heard many false confessions from the bench. Tough guys mostly. They change their minds and recant, but by then it's too late. I don't think your guy did it."

They started to walk. "Has the gun been found?" Jim asked.

"Not yet."

Pat joined Jim for dinner at his house. Jim said little. Pat knew what that meant: he was turning ideas over in his head, ideas which he tried out on Pat as they cleared the dishes.

"Tell me how this sounds to you. The shooter jumps on the bus at Beauty Shop Row. He fires two quick shots, hops off the bus and vanishes in the side streets. He chose that stop to get on because he knows the streets, knows the shops, knows the houses. I'll bet he lives in the area."

"Sounds reasonable," Pat replied. "Amateur or professional?"

"Amateur. No doubt in my mind."

"Why so certain?"

"The kid was visibly jittery. I don't think he was used to guns, let alone shooting people in the head. It all happened so fast, a lot didn't register until I replayed the shooting, over and over. Only then could I see the kid's mouth quivering as if he were about to sob."

It still was light outside, but darkness was closing in earlier and earlier. Before long, when they ate in his kitchen, the blue sky out the windows would turn black by the end of dinner.

"I have to pretend I'm the killer. Think like he thought. Care to get your hair done?"

Pat was used to Jim's non-sequiturs.

"Are you suggesting a field trip?"

"To Beauty Shop Row, yes."

Pat had low maintenance hair, rarely had her hair done, considered it a useless indulgence.

"Don't you already know that stretch of street?"

"Not as a killer. I have to get inside his head, think like he thinks."

"I'll pass. I'll buy something for dinner while you're on your field trip."

Cambridge Street between Harvard and MIT was pre-gentrification. Vying for space with Rosie's and the other beauty shops were a wire transfer store, a Portuguese social club, a Caribbean grocery store, a storefront insurance office, and the occasional multi-family house. Jim had a toy town when he was a boy – a toy town is what East Cambridge looked like to Jim as he walked it. Was there anything about it per se that would make a potential killer on the Lechmere bus say, "this must be the place"? Could resentment of the universities at either end have anything to do with the shooting? But why take out your resentment on a Haitian-American bus driver if that were the case? Jim would stick with his original theory: that the shooter chose to hop onto the bus on Beauty Shop Row because he knew the nooks and crannies – the hiding places – of the neighborhood.

"What did you conclude from your field trip?" Pat asked Jim when she walked through the front door carrying a paper bag.

"About what?"

"Do you think Beauty Shop Row had anything to do with Ricardo Abbé's murder?"

"No. I think the streets surrounding it did, but not the shops of the Row themselves. What's in the bag you're carrying?"

"Dinner. Remember?"

Pat stashed the groceries in Jim's kitchen and returned to the living room.

"Jim, you've done great so far as an amateur sleuth, but your winning streak can't last forever."

"Why not?"

"Don't be hurt. All I'm saying is you're human."

"How dare you? Wash your mouth out."

Pat came over and sat on Jim's lap. "Dinner or sex?"

Jim chuckled. "Do I have to choose one?"

"To be first, unless you want to eat while we're having sex."

"Get off my lap so I can make up my mind without distraction."

She stood. "That's it. I'll cook while you decide."

"No, I've decided."

"Too late." Pat blew Jim a kiss while she headed to the kitchen.

6

Ted Conover was normally a buttoned-up custodian of the law, but sitting behind his desk the next day he seemed to be trying his best to suppress a case of ebullience.

"I wanted you to hear this from me before you read about it in the *Globe*. Francois Benoit will go on trial next month for the murder of Ricardo Abbé. He will be represented by a public defender, Carol Vincent. I've seen her at work and she's good."

The early morning sun was breaking and entering through Ted's office windows. Jim had to squint to see Ted past the glare. "Thanks for the heads up, Ted, but I'm not going to quit looking for the man I saw pull the trigger – and it's not Francois Benoit."

Ted shrugged. "You'll be wasting your time." He looked at his watch. "I'm arguing a case of spousal abuse in thirty minutes and I want to review my notes."

"You need thirty minutes?"

Ted made a brushing motion with his hand. "Get out. Scram."

Jim walked the short distance to the Lechmere T station to wait for a bus home. Ted had sounded unusually sure of himself, which gave Jim pause. Ted was not a man to make careless judgements. All Jim had were a glance and a hunch.

He sat on a bench to wait for the bus. The Lechmere station was slated to be torn down and rebuilt closer to a rapidly rising complex of office towers and apartments, but for now the station remained a decrepit wooden remnant of old Cambridge. The Green Line subway and several bus lines including the #69 converged there.

As he sat reviewing what Ted had said, he felt someone sit down beside him on the bench. Whoever it was took up a considerable amount of space and he sensed that it was a woman.

The woman's leg jiggled. "Can you believe this? Has the #69 bus ever been on time? I'm sick of this. Know what I mean?"

Jim glanced her way. His bench mate was the pink-haired woman who almost knocked him down when she careened out of Rosie's House of Beauty.

When Jim didn't immediately answer, the woman leveled her gaze and sputtered, "Yes, you, I'm talking to you."

"I take it you don't remember me," Jim said calmly.

"Remember you? Why should I? Do you think I remember everyone I meet? I meet a lot of people. *Important* people." A #69 bus to Harvard was approaching. The woman got to her feet. "Why should I remember *you*?"

The bus pulled to a stop in front of the woman. It didn't genuflect, which Jim took as a sign. "I'm the man you almost knocked over in front of Rosie's."

The pink-haired woman studied Jim scornfully. "You'll have to do better than that. Still don't remember."

She climbed onto the bus and sat across from the driver. Jim followed her and sat directly behind the driver. Once the bus was underway, the woman barked nonstop at the driver, who took no note of her. Jim wondered if she had ridden on this driver's bus before, or if she harangued every driver she rode with.

The woman got off at Beauty Shop Row, and Jim wondered if she was returning to Rosie's. He remembered Rosie's owner standing in the doorway and shouting at her not to come back. Jim resisted the urge to follow her to see where she was going.

*

Sasha Cohen asked to meet with Jim at The Long Gone tomorrow. "8 a.m.?"

He arrived before Sasha and threw caution to the winds, ordering a Ethiopian Super Natural which he'd never tried before. To paraphrase Flaubert – be stodgy in one's habits so one can be bold at The Long Gone.

"You're looking troubled this morning," he said to Sasha when she arrived.

"I am. I'm going to be covering the Benoit trial."

"Why does that trouble you?"

"I've looked into Benoit. He's a bad actor but I don't think he did this crime."

"Neither do I."

"That's what I wanted to hear. You saw the shooting."

"And I saw the lineup where Benoit was picked as the shooter by several other riders on the bus and still I doubt it's him."

"Knowing you, you're not going to give up."

"I am not, and you can help me by putting me in touch with your colleagues who cover East Cambridge. I think the answer lies there."

It didn't take Sasha long to come back with a name: Dave Fitzpatrick, who wrote a weekly column called Bits and Pieces, which focused on street life in Cambridge, Somerville, Malden, and Medford. Fitzpatrick had been with the *Globe* for six years, before which he worked for the Cambridge *Chronicle*.

They met in the food court of the Cambridgeside Galleria, an indoor shopping mall that once upon a time had been trendy. Fitzpatrick, a weathered man in his fifties, looked as untrendy as the mall. A man who got right to the point. "I hear you're interested in East Cambridge. My modus operandi is to talk to the locals, and the ferocity of complaints by East Cambridge residents always makes me smile. They love and hate their neighborhood in equal measure."

"Any complaint in particular?"

"Newcomers. They can't stand newcomers even though they or their ancestors were newcomers once upon a time. And the city of Cambridge, which according to the residents of East Cambridge does far more for Harvard and MIT than for ordinary citizens. And the MBTA, which doesn't clean its buses often enough. Etc, etc, but for God's sake, don't make changes. They like their neighborhood as it is. Covering East Cambridge bolsters my amused belief in the irrationality of the human race."

"What's the speculation among the residents about the murder of the bus driver?"

"Everybody has an opinion, but there isn't a consensus. Not a professional hit job is the closest thing to a consensus." Fitzpatrick hadn't touched his coffee. He did so now. "Cold. I talk too much."

"Does the street think the man who has been indicted for the murder is guilty?"

"Benoit? No, the scuttlebutt is that a mistake is being made. I'm inclined to think that the murder had its origins in personal payback. If you identify the killer, I'll give you a big shoutout in my column."

"Which I can do without, thanks."

"Actually, you'd make a good subject for a column even if you don't solve the crime – Judge Turns Sleuth. What do you say?"

"Ask Sasha, she'll tell you, I have plenty of ego but the personality of a recluse. Thanks but no thanks."

Fitzpatrick gave a smile and a shrug. "If you change your mind."

"Final question. Does the scuttlebutt believe there is an epicenter to the murder?"

"The tightknit residential streets that huddle together off Cambridge Street."

"That's what I think, too."

Thoughts without shape or form, but with some connection to each other, were organizing themselves in Jim's mind.

Fitzpatrick was speaking to him. "Will you keep me informed of your progress?"

"If the circumstances permit, I will. How about you? Will you keep me informed?"

"Deal." Fitzpatrick stood and offered his hand.

The Cambridgeside Galleria, where Jim and Fitz-patrick had met, was on the banks of the Charles. The river formed a basin there, and Jim liked to walk beside the basin when he worked in the courthouse. Across the river, Mass General Hospital stood ready to admit him when he had his heart attack, aneurism, or stroke.

Jim stayed at Pat's that night and walked home in the morning. Beauty Shop Row looked its best in the early morning. There was something about cool sunlight that brought out the best in the Row. The purple neon sign of Rosie's House of Beauty's looked stylish not garish. Jim smiled as he saw a young man sprinting to catch a Lechmere bus. Jim felt good physically. He could sprint if he had to.

The bus pulled away from the curb, affording Jim a glimpse of the sprinting young man taking a rear seat. The young man in profile looked familiar, but it was only after the bus pulled away that it clicked in Jim's brain who the young man resembled.

Jim wanted to catch up with the bus but he wasn't young enough in spite of how good he felt. Anyway, what were the chances of the young man actually being the shooter? There were scores of dark-haired young men with furtive eyes in Cambridge. Jim had only caught a glimpse of the shooter the day of the murder, and all hell had broken loose after the shooting making positive identification all but impossible. But he couldn't shake the conviction that he had just seen the shooter again.

His first call was to Ted. "I'm sorry, Judge Randall. Mr. Conover is in court. Would you like his voicemail?"

"Please."

After the beep, Jim left his message. "Ted, you'll ridicule me, but I think I just saw Ricardo Abbé's killer get on the #69 bus at the same stop where Abbé was shot, returning to the scene of the crime as it were. It reinforces my belief that you've got the wrong guy."

Next call was to Pat.

"I'm a genius. I just solved the murder of the bus driver."

"Congratulations."

"I saw the killer get on the #69 bus at a stop on Beauty Show Row."

"Okay."

"I understand why you are skeptical, but I'll bet the young man lives nearby."

"Jim, would you accept your identification of him in court if you were still a judge?"

"Of course not, but that's the beauty of being a sleuth instead of a judge."

"I'll come to your house tonight."

"Eager to change the subject, are we?"

"When you get frustrated, you tend to drift off into outer space."

"Wait and see. A critical mass is forming in my brain. The ah-ha! moment is approaching."

"You don't have 'ah-ha!' moments, nor 'eureka!' moments, Jim, you have moments of quiet relief."

"You've just given me a title for my memoir."

"Which you will never write."

"Correct. But if I ever do, *Moments Of Quiet Relief – Memoirs of a Former Judge*, will be the title."

7

Carol Vincent's phone call the next morning caught Jim by surprise.

"Good morning, Judge. I'm the public defender who has been assigned to represent Francois Benoit. I understand from the DA's office that you witnessed the shooting, is that correct?"

Carol Vincent had a down-to-earth voice, the voice of a person hard to catch off-guard.

"Yes, I did."

"Will you testify in court as to what you saw?"

"Of course, and I'm willing to say I have doubts your client is the man who shot Ricardo Abbé, but I'm not willing to say under oath that he isn't. As you may have heard, I am investigating the case on my own and I haven't reached a firm conclusion."

"I've heard you have a reputation for unorthodox detecting methods."

"You mean, I guess a lot?"

Carol Vincent chuckled. "Doesn't everybody? Some people just pretend they don't."

Pat overheard part of the conversation. "Who was that?" she asked when Jim got off the phone.

"Carol Vincent, the public defender who is representing the man charged with murdering Ricardo Abbé."

"She wants you to testify, correct?"

"Yes. I don't like to oppose Ted in open court, but I will if she wants me to. Her client is innocent."

Jim stayed away from the trial until Carol Vincent's call. In lieu of attending, he got reports from Sasha, who covered the trial for the *Globe*.

"Your friend Ted Conover is a very able lawyer," Sasha reported after opening arguments.

"I know. I presided over many trials in which Ted represented the Commonwealth. What was the gist of his argument?"

"Multiple eyewitnesses, security cameras in the bus, facial recognition software, an alibi that proved to be false. Strong case."

"And Carol Vincent's rebuttal?"

"She did the best she could. She argued the unreliability of eyewitness testimony, especially in traumatic circumstances. She argued the newness of facial recognition as a forensic tool, and she argued that the defendant's false alibi suggested that he was a liar, but did not prove that he was a murderer, i.e., she was good but not as effective as your friend Ted, in my opinion."

"Ted's an experienced litigator, one of the best."

The prosecution's questioning of witnesses took two days. Jim was called to testify for the defense on the third day. He entered the courtroom feeling as if he had never set foot in a courtroom before, his head empty of twenty-one years of experience as a judge and of any stoicism he may once have possessed. He mounted the witness stand with trepidation.

"Raise your right hand. Do you solemnly swear to tell the truth, the whole truth, and nothing but the truth, so help you God?"

"I do."

"Be seated."

Jim surveyed the courtroom: at the prosecutor's table, Ted sifted through his papers; Francois Benoit at the defense table looked sullen and scared; Ricardo Abbé's widow watched intently from the spectator rows; Sasha Cohen took notes in the front row; the twelve men and women of the jury were poised to do their duty. Sitting in the rear of the courtroom was the pink-haired woman who had almost knocked Jim over on Beauty Shop Row.

He didn't have time to assess the meaning of her presence because Carol Vincent was approaching the witness stand.

"Good morning, Judge Randall."

"Good morning."

"You were a judge on the Massachusetts Superior Court for twenty-one years, is that correct?"

"It is. I retired when I turned sixty-five, 4 years ago."

"In your capacity as a judge you presided over many, many trials, I presume."

"Yes. Both civil and criminal."

"Which meant you heard many witnesses testify?"

"Many."

"And you studied the witnesses as part of assessing their credibility, would that be fair to say?"

"Of course."

Carol Vincent turned towards the jury box, the confident way she moved saying there was no need to rush. "You were a passenger on Ricardo Abbé's bus the morning he was shot to death, is that correct?"

"It is."

"Did you have a clear view of the shooting?"

"Unobstructed, from beginning to end, yes."

Vincent approached the jury box. "Please describe to the jury what you saw."

From the judge's bench Jim had watched countless jurors listen to testimony. Occasionally a juror would grimace, squirm or frown, but most the time, jurors remained stone-faced. Testifying now as a witness, he thought he saw skepticism, impatience, and who-are-you-kidding written on the jurors' faces. He liked the view from the judge's bench better.

His throat needed clearing. "I ride the Lechmere bus often enough to have seen Ricardo Abbé, the driver, more than once. He struck me as a man who took pride in his job, a quiet man who didn't make trouble, so it came as a complete shock when a young man wearing wraparound sunglasses and a knit cap pulled low over his forehead, jumped on the bus and fired two shots into Mr. Abbé's head."

A woman juror winced.

"Before anyone could react, the young man jumped off the bus and disappeared. After a brief moment of shocked silence, there was complete chaos on the bus, screams, shouts, a rush for the doors. I spent years on the bench doing my best to keep a level head when all others were losing theirs, but I, too, panicked. I should've called 911 but I didn't until I was off the bus. Someone more level headed than I did, thank God, but it did no good because Mr. Abbé was dead when the EMT's arrived."

Carol Vincent allowed a pause before continuing. "Judge Randall, how close were you to the shooter?"

"I was sitting three rows from the front door, across from a man in a wheelchair who had been helped onto the bus by Mr. Abbé. Mr. Abbé had just returned to the driver's seat when the shooting occurred."

"So you got a good look at the shooter?"

"Much of his face was obscured, but I got a good look at him."

Carol Vincent stepped aside. "Judge Randall, is the shooter in the courtroom today?"

"No, he is not." Jim heard an intake of breath – from the jury? the spectators?

"You're sure? Take a good look."

Jim swept his eyes over the courtroom. "I'm sure."

"How about the defendant, Francois Benoit? Take a close look."

"The defendant is not the man I saw shoot Ricardo Abbé."

"Thank you. No further questions."

"Your turn, Mr. Conover," the judge said.

Ted stood and buttoned his suit coat. "Thank you, Your Honor. Judge Randall, for the record, we have known each other a long time."

"Correct. For over twenty years."

"For the most part we like each other, correct?"

Jim smiled a Judge Randall smile, a smile hard to interpret but bearing no malice. "I can't speak for how you feel about me, but I like you okay." A giggle came from somewhere in the courtroom.

"Judge Randall, you have testified that you didn't see the shooter in either of the lineups you viewed, yet the man the Commonwealth is charging with the murder was picked out of a lineup by several other riders on the bus. You were the only eyewitness out of seven who didn't pick him."

"And they may be right. Eyewitness testimony, including mine, is notoriously subject to error, but in my opinion the defendant did not kill Mr. Abbé."

"And we all respect your opinion, Judge Randall, however wrong it may be. I have no further questions of this witness."

Carol Vincent stood. "In effect, Judge Randall, you were a professional witness watcher for twenty-one years, watching witnesses as they testified, studying their faces, listening to their voices, and in your opinion the defendant in this case is not the shooter. Correct?"

"Yes."

"No further questions, Your Honor."

Jim was the last witness for the day. To decompress, Jim sat on a bench in the vest pocket park outside the courthouse. How strange, he thought: while I was testifying, I felt like I was the one on trial. Sitting on a park bench outside the courthouse, I feel as if I've just escaped from prison.

He saw Ted walk from the courthouse and hurried to catch up.

Ted stopped when he saw Jim trotting towards him. "Slow down. I don't want to be responsible for your heart attack."

"I'll sign a disclaimer. Any chance you're heading to Ipsa Loquitur?"

"No, but I like the idea."

They walked together silently until they reached the bar. Once inside, Jim couldn't stop talking.

"How'd I do?" he began.

"You did fine, Jim. Are we still friends?"

"Of course. You may be a shitty lawyer, but you're a good friend."

Ted signaled to the waitress. "Red wine for my cantankerous friend, Long Trail IPA for me."

"I felt outnumbered while I testified," Jim said.

"You had reason. 6-1."

"But I still think you've got the wrong guy."

"I understand."

"I have a question."

"Shoot. Poor choice of words. Sorry."

"Did you notice a pink-haired woman sitting in the rear of the courtroom?"

"I did. I've seen her before. She's a court watcher, attends a lot of trials. I'm sure you had a few in your courtroom."

"From time to time."

"Why do you ask?"

"Lately I've seen her in the neighborhood where the murder took place. On the Lechmere bus, on the sidewalk of Beauty Shop Row, on a bench at the Lechmere T station.

And now at the trial of the accused killer of Ricardo Abbé. There's something about her. I can't shake the feeling she's complicit."

"Knowing how stodgy you are, I assume she sticks in your mind because of her pink hair."

"In case you're interested, I know where she has her hair done. Rosie's House of Beauty, near the bus stop where the shooter got on. That's where I first encountered her, screaming at her hairdresser."

"Okay," Ted said, elongating the word as much as possible.

Jim shrugged. "I know, I know, what does that prove? Very little to nothing, but I have a feeling about her."

Ted reached over and put his hand on Jim's shoulder. "You're losing it, my friend. Oh, good, here are our drinks. Cheers." They clicked glasses.

"Let's make a bet about Benoit's guilt or innocence," Jim said.

"Are you nuts? Do you *like* losing money?"

"Put up or shut up."

"Okay, $10," Ted said.

"How about $100?"

"You're insane."

"How about it? $100 that your guy isn't the killer."

Ted shrugged. "If you insist." He held out his hand for Jim to shake. "You're on."

It was a short walk across the river to Pat's. How old would he have to be before walking became a chore rather than a pleasure? The surface of the Charles was dark, lending weight to the water.

Pat called out, "Jim?" when she heard him unlock her door.

"Yes, it's me."

She appeared at the door. "How did it go?"

"As well as could be expected. I felt like a criminal while I was testifying."

"Come sit in the living room, I'll pour the wine."

He sat in his favorite chair in her living room. The universe righted itself and by the time Pat emerged from the kitchen with two glasses of wine, he realized the chair had officially become one of his safe places. He didn't add safe places to his list very often, so this was a big deal. Perhaps a brief christening ceremony?

"Tell me more." She sat on the sofa across from him.

He sipped the wine she had handed him. "Is this new?"

"Yes, do you like it?"

"I'm afraid to say yes, because then you'll tell me it's from the Bronx or Queens."

"I wouldn't pull that on you. No, it's French, but we haven't had it before."

He took another sip. "From the Roussillon?"

"Very good. I'm impressed."

He hoisted the glass. "I felt uncomfortable on the witness stand today, as if I would be found out. Testifying is intimidating, even for a former judge."

"I've never had the pleasure," Pat said.

Jim took a long breath. "I never want to move from this chair. Can you bring me all my meals from now on?"

"Of course."

"And run my baths."

"You don't take baths, you shower."

"There you go again, always the pragmatist."

They went to the bistro at the base of the hill for dinner. All the tables were full, so they ate at the bar.

"One interesting thing I learned from Ted today is that the pink- haired woman I literally and figuratively keep running into is a court watcher."

"Was she in the courtroom today?"

"Yes."

"Did you ever see her in your courtroom?"

"Not that I remember."

"You'd remember a pink-haired woman."

"Not all of her hair is pink, only the tips."

Pat smiled.

"Why is that funny?"

"It isn't. You are."

The attorneys made their closing arguments the next morning. Both attorneys were good – Ted of course, but also the public defender, Carol Vincent. Then the judge ordered the jury to begin deliberations. The jury was still deliberating when court adjourned for the night.

Jim was fidgety that evening. "I'm nervous," he said. "More nervous than when I was a presiding judge."

"Why?" Pat said.

"You tell me."

"Because you lack control over what happens."

The jury deliberated for two days and two nights. Jim wanted to be in the courtroom to hear the verdict when it was announced. Pat came with him. Jim was glad she was there.

The courtroom was crowded. Among the spectators was the pink-haired woman.

The judge ordered the bailiff to summon the jury. A moment later, the jurors filed into the courtroom, looking solemn. When the jury was seated, the judge asked the defendant to rise.

"Mr. Foreperson, has the jury reached a verdict?"

"It has, Your Honor." He handed a folded piece of paper to a bailiff, who in turn handed it to the judge. The judge carefully unfolded it, read it, and handed it back to the foreperson.

"In the case of Commonwealth v. Benoit, the defendant is charged with murder in the second degree. How does the jury find?"

"We find the defendant guilty as charged."

"So say you all?"

One by one, the jurors answered in the affirmative.

The defendant looked disbelieving. He had recanted his confession soon after he made it and apparently couldn't believe that hadn't been enough to clear him.

The judge continued. "Members of the jury, the Commonwealth thanks you for your service. Now that your service is over, you are free to discuss this case with anyone you please, but I would remind you of what is at stake and urge you to be discreet in what you say and to whom you say it."

Jim watched the jurors file out of the jury box, a scene he had watched hundreds of times but which never failed to move him. Judge not lest ye be judged, unless you are a member of a jury, then judge ye must.

When the jury had left the courtroom, the judge announced that sentencing would take place at 9 am the following day and adjourned the court for the night.

Jim and Pat waited until the courtroom was cleared before they headed for the exit. One of the long serving bailiffs said hello to them as they left, "Two judges for the price of one. My lucky day."

Pat replied, "How's the family, George?"

"Still annoying the hell out of me."

Second degree murder carries with it a sentence of life in prison with the possibility of parole after a term of years left to the discretion of the judge. Jim told himself not to grieve too much for Benoit, after all a jury had found him guilty and all Jim had to counter that with were a glimpse and a hunch.

Pat stayed with Jim at his townhouse that night. He felt drained and looked forward to the comfort of his own bed. What more could he have done to prevent what he considered a miscarriage of justice?

"There wasn't anything you could have done, Jim," Pat said when he voiced his frustration.

"There's always something that can be done. I didn't try hard enough."

"Don't beat yourself up."

Jim rarely slept through a night; he fell asleep quickly, then woke later with a head full of clutter. Pat always slept soundly. He marveled at how quiet and still she was when she slept. He wasn't that quiet and still, ever – awake or asleep. If he wasn't snoring, he was breathing heavily, as if breathing were hard. His ribs were sore from Pat elbowing him in the side to shush him.

He awoke while it was still dark, got dressed, and was at the courthouse when the doors opened. He had two hours to kill before sentencing, so he sat on a bench in the lobby and waited.

The courtroom doors opened at a quarter to nine. By that time, Jim wasn't alone. Sasha Cohen had arrived moments before, and the pink-haired woman arrived just as the doors opened.

Jim picked a row close to the front of the courtroom. As Benoit was led into the courtroom by the side door, he beseeched the onlookers with his eyes. Rarely had Jim seen a more defeated man. He briefly sat down at the defense table, then arose for the sentencing: life in prison, with the possibility of parole after twenty-five years. Only then did Benoit physically falter, his legs seeming to buckle. Two bailiffs grabbed him by the arms and led him out of the courtroom.

The bang of a gavel and twenty-five years in prison. Over and out.

Jim turned to go. The pink-haired woman had already left the courtroom and so too had Sasha. Jim walked into the hallway. After the claustrophobia of the courtroom, the hallway felt like the great outdoors. A few stragglers remained; some court watchers can't tear themselves away from courtrooms even when a trial isn't in session

As Jim exited the building, he saw the pink-haired woman haranguing a young man in front of the courthouse. The young man had been waiting for her, by the looks of it. He was in his late teens and looked familiar. The pink-haired woman was stabbing him in the chest with her finger: "See? You had nothing to worry about! Didn't I tell you? Didn't I? Always listen to your mother." Stab, stab, stab. As Jim drew near, the pink-haired woman realized she was being overheard and hovered her finger mid-stab. "What the hell are you looking at?" she growled at Jim.

"Good to see you again, ma'am. Remember me? We keep running into each other. Is this your son?"

"What business is that of yours?"

Jim extended his hand to the young man. "Hello, I'm Judge Randall."

The young man turned his head away. "I know who you are."

"And I know you, not by name but by sight. If I'm not mistaken, I've seen you on the Lechmere bus."

The young man tugged on his mother's arm. "Come on, Ma. We gotta go."

Jim followed at a discrete distance. Jim's body was not built for shadowing a young man and his mother, but Jim knew the streets of East Cambridge well enough to stay out of their sight without losing sight of them. He followed them from the courthouse the short distance to the maze of residential streets off Beauty Shop Row – parking-by-permit only streets, street cleaning once a month streets. He followed as mother and son turned onto East Canton Street and climbed the front steps of a pale blue house with yellow trim and two front doors. He watched from a safe distance as they closed one of the front doors behind them. A moment later, a second floor light flicked on.

The house number was 49B – 49B East Canton Street – a block from the house where Ricardo Abbé had lived and his widow still did. Jim pulled his phone from his pocket and texted a question to Ernie Farrell – Who lives at 49B East Canton Street, Cambridge?

Jim put the phone away and walked to the bus stop, where he waited for the always tardy, extremely frustrating, ultimately reliable bus.

Ernie's reply was waiting for Jim when he got home.

Muriel Watkins, fifty-
two, divorced. Two kids.
Connie, twenty-seven,
divorced, lives in San Mateo,
California. Timothy, eighteen,
a graduating senior at
Cambridge Rindge and Latin
High School, lives with his
mother at 49B East Canton
Street. Helpful?

Jim's reply:

Very. Thanks.

Pat spent the night at Jim's place. They ate leftovers and drank stale wine; Jim didn't notice that the wine was stale, which had never, in Pat's memory, happened before. When she mentioned the spoiled wine to Jim, he seemed startled. "Really?"

"Do you want to tell me what's going through your head, although I can guess. It has to do with the jailing of a man you believe to be innocent."

Jim picked up the thread without missing a beat. "And seeing the pink-haired woman in the courtroom, and afterwards seeing her berating a young man who I believe to be her son and who I believe I saw fire two bullets into Ricardo Abbé's brain."

"Wow."

"There's more. Mother and son live a few houses from Ricardo Abbé's widow."

"Don't tell me you followed them."

"I did. Stealthily, I must add, thereby adding another tool to my amateur sleuth's tool kit."

"Don't look smug. You should have called the police."

"What good would that have done? In their minds, the killer has been caught and convicted."

"Or called Ted Conover."

"Again, as much as I like and admire Ted, he and I have a fundamental disagreement on this case."

"So what are you going to do? You're not going to become a stalker, are you?"

"Retired judges do not stalk. We are too dignified. We may trail, we may follow, but we do not stalk. I simply can't let an innocent man spend the next twenty-five years in prison."

8

Misha Abbé refused to meet when Jim called. "To what purpose? My husband's killer is in jail. What good would meeting again do?"

"I understand how you feel," Jim replied over the phone, "but I have serious doubts the right man is in jail."

"Really?"

"Yes, really."

"But you told the police you didn't get a good look at the man who shot my Ricardo."

"True, I didn't, but in spite of his sunglasses and knit cap, I could tell he was baby-faced. His lips quivered after he pulled the trigger and for an instant I thought he might cry. I got a good look at Benoit in court. His face is hardened. Do you know Muriel Watkins?"

Misha Abbé normally spoke in even tones, but the mention of Muriel Watkins made her sputter. "Know her? Who on this street doesn't? She's loud, obnoxious, and vulgar. I avoid her when I can."

"How about her son, Timothy? Do you know him?"

"Only a little. He is as quiet as his mother is loud. I believe he's in high school."

"Did he or his mother ever have words with your husband?"

"She had words with everybody on the block. I'm sorry, Judge Randall, but I need to grieve my husband. Please leave me alone."

Jim had called Mrs. Abbé from his kitchen. When he got off his phone, he climbed to his study on the third floor. Settled in his reading chair, he stared out the window. The weather had been mild for weeks, but any experienced New Englander could spot the signs of impending winter. Bare branches could be seen through the sparse leaves on the trees.

He needed more information from two very different women, one of whom, Mrs. Abbé, had flatly refused. Muriel Watkins was the other. Fat chance. Why would she incriminate herself or her son? Perhaps he could take advantage of her temper to get her to blurt something incriminating, but that was a long shot.

He stood from his chair. This isn't like you, he said to himself. Make up your mind, all in or all out. Don't dither.

He returned downstairs, donned his autumn jacket and left the house. The outside air felt good. He walked to the end of his street and waited to cross. While he waited, a Lechmere bus pulled to a stop in front of the high school – which he took as a sign, good or bad, he wasn't sure.

His intended destination was a bench in the library park where he could watch the front door of the high school. The bench he chose got good sun, cool but bright. He had occupied a judicial bench for twenty-one years, now he occupied a bench in a public park hoping to see a student named Tim Watkins emerge from the high school. Not the career arc he had in mind when he went to law school.

Confirming that portents do come true, Tim Watkins emerged from the high school talking to a young woman.

He was laughing and self-conscious in equal measure. When he spotted Jim, he seemed rattled.

Jim stayed on the bench, watching. He watched as Tim said something to the young woman that made her look in Jim's direction, and watched as Tim hopped on the Lechmere bus. Only then did Jim rise from the bench and walk back home.

*

Pat joined Jim at his house for the night. She was skeptical when Jim told her what he had done that morning. "You sat and watched hoping you'd see young Watkins? Doesn't that make you a stalker?"

"Not at all. Stalking implies movement. I accomplished my purpose while sitting still. Economy of effort."

What exactly *did* you accomplish?"

"Come on, Pat. You know."

"Humor me."

"I let Timothy know by my presence that the conviction of Francois Benoit hasn't closed the case for me. I was prepared to speak to him, but when I saw how rattled he got when he spotted me, I decided I had accomplished my purpose."

"Jim, given how explosive Muriel Watkins is, you risk being accused of harassing her son."

"By sitting on a park bench?"

"I'm saying, watch your step. Don't get carried away."

"Okay, I accept the warning. I'm flying blind and that could lead to a crash."

"I'm hungry."

"Me too. How about the Italian place across the Yard? We haven't been there in months."

The young man who greeted them at the door rarely smiled but was always gracious.

"Good to see you, Judge Randall, Judge Knowles. It's been a while. I've put you at a window table." He plucked two menus off the upright desk and escorted Jim and Pat to the window wall of the restaurant. "Enjoy."

Jim scanned the menu. "When did 'enjoy' become the word of choice in restaurants?"

"What's wrong with 'enjoy'?"

"What if I don't 'want' to enjoy? What if I want to be 'miserable' while I eat?"

"Poor Jim."

Jim much preferred French to Italian wine, but Italian wines were his second choice. He ordered a carafe of Sangiovese.

"What do you hope to achieve by planting seeds of doubt in young Watkins's mind?" Pat asked while they waited for the wine.

"Keep mother and son on edge until one of them makes a mistake."

"How long will that take?"

"I don't have a playbook. I'll push here, push there until I get a reaction. According to Misha Abbé and my own observations, Muriel Watkins is a hot head, and hot heads are more likely to lose control."

"But why the son?"

"He's not a hot head or a hardened criminal, but if I'm right that he pulled the trigger, he's got the most to lose and the weakest defenses."

The wine arrived. "Do you like it?" Jim asked after Pat tried it.

"Yes. It's nice." She put her glass down. "Jim, I love how your mind works, but to *my* mind, this is a leap too far. There is no evidence that the son had anything to do with the shooting."

"Only my own eyes, and the rattled way he's been acting since he knows I'm on to him."

"Stalking him, perhaps?"

Jim held up a finger to silence her. "I just thought of something."

"What?"

Jim extracted his phone and started texting. His thumbs hit more than one key no matter how careful he was, so he tapped the keys with his index finger. It took time.

"Will you be finished by desert?"

"If you give me a hard time, I'll slow down." He tapped a moment longer then looked up from the keys. "Marcus Jackson."

"Excuse me?"

"I'm texting Marcus Jackson, the high school student who helped me at the beginning of this case."

*

Marcus agreed to meet at the upscale sandwich shop around the corner from Jim's house. The shop was more Harvard than high school, and Marcus looked self-conscious when he joined Jim at a table. "I've never been here before," was the first thing he said when he sat down.

"It's an older crowd," Jim replied.

Marcus looked around at the laptops and white faces. "No, it's not that. I don't fit in, know what I mean?"

"Then I'm especially grateful you agreed to meet with me. You may know that a young man named Benoit was convicted of Ricardo Abbé's murder."

"Everybody knows."

"I don't think he's the killer. I think there was a rush to judgement."

Marcus narrowed his eyes. "You don't quit, do you?"

"No, I do not."

"Okay, so what do you want from me this time?"

"Answers to a few more questions."

Marcus shifted his weight. His tall, skinny frame didn't fit the chair. His eyes simultaneously conveyed sweet and sour – a young man afraid to reveal his vulnerable side. "I'm ready."

"Where you and your mother live on East Canton Street is near the Abbé's, if I remember correctly?"

Marcus nodded.

"Which means you also live near Muriel Watkins and her son, Tim."

"Yes, diagonally across the street."

"I've gotten to know Muriel Watkins a little. I can see how she could be an obnoxious neighbor."

Marcus hooted. "Obnoxious? Yelling at everyone on the street, especially anyone who isn't white, saying she's better than us, smarter than us. She hates me, says I've got a big mouth. Obnoxious? I guess you could call her that."

"Is it a white-versus-black thing?"

"Who knows? I think it's just an asshole thing."

"What's your impression of Tim, her son?"

"He's okay. I don't know him well. We live on the same street, go to the same school, but he keeps to himself."

"Is he like his mother?"

"Hell, no! Tim's the quietest kid I know. I feel sorry for him, with a mother like that. I'll bet she takes out her temper on him."

"Do you know that for a fact?"

"No, just my sense of how spooked he is. No one is that spooked unless he's been treated real bad."

"What's the consensus at your school about Benoit being the shooter?"

Marcus took his time answering. "Judge, the kids who ride the Lechmere bus liked Mr. Abbé. We could tease him." Long pause, big shrug. "We want to believe his killer is behind bars, but the consensus is the cops needed a scapegoat."

"Thank you, Marcus. I appreciate your willingness to help me." Jim handed Marcus his card. "If you or any of your friends have more to say, please contact me."

Marcus looked years older than he did when he walked in. "No problem."

Jim sat thinking for what seemed a long time, but when he looked at his watch, he realized only twenty minutes had passed since Marcus walked into the coffee shop. Jim had trouble reading Marcus, but talking to him again had given Jim at least a glimmer of understanding: Marcus wanted to be honest but didn't want to appear naive; Jim could trust what he said, but shouldn't take every word he said at face value.

Of one thing Jim was sure: Marcus wanted Ricardo Abbé's killer behind bars as much if not more than Jim did. They both had a stake in catching the killer. Jim had seen the murder; Marcus respected Ricardo Abbé from years of riding on his bus.

Jim spent the night at Pat's Beacon Hill apartment. Her apartment was spacious but on one floor. Jim's townhouse felt cramped on any one floor but had three. Vertical versus horizontal living. On such weighty matters did Jim's idle mind dwell.

He loved eating in Pat's kitchen. If there were one room in his life that most felt like home, it would be her kitchen. Most of that was due to Pat's presence; any room she was in felt like home.

Not for the first time, he asked himself, why not move in together? Why spend any nights apart? He had asked himself this question before, and every time had arrived at the same answer: because occasional solitude suited them both. If they hadn't spent years alone after their spouses died, it might be different.

Pat cooked a kind of chicken he liked very much. "What do you call this?"

"Chicken."

"I mean...oh, never mind. I wouldn't remember if you told me."

"How did Marcus Jackson react to you?"

"He wants to find the answer as much as I do."

"Does he trust you?"

"Good question. I don't know. Probably. At least a little."

"I know you're torturing a theory about the killing and you've hinted at what it is, but why don't you just tell me?"

"You're right, as always. Or usually. I'm not going to admit you're always right."

"So what's your theory?"

"I'm convinced more than ever that when the truth is known, the pink-haired woman will be at the heart of it. I don't know why I'm so sure."

"Because she almost knocked you over outside Rosie's. That to you was a metaphor, a clue," Pat said.

"Who do you think was the killer?"

"I side with Ted. My money's on Benoit."

"That would make my life simpler."

"But also mean you were wrong."

"I don't mind being shown up. I'm not thin skinned."

"You don't? You're not? Could've fooled me."

"A foolish consistency is the hobgoblin of little minds, to quote Emerson."

"Funny, I never thought of you as a transcendentalist."

"I am a man of many guises."

Pat sighed. "Whatever happened to the steady, slightly boring judge in the courtroom next to mine? I miss that guy at times."

"Slightly boring? Is that what you thought of me when we were on the bench?"

"Jim, I adored you. Still do for some reason."

"Admit it, you love my joie de vivre."

Pat laughed out loud. "Joie de vivre?"

Jim feigned innocence. "What's so funny?"

"Nothing. Nothing at all." Pat laughed harder. "Sorry. Can't help it."

9

First stop the next day was Rosie's House Of Beauty.

He had never been inside before. The interior was crimson and chrome, as garish as the purple neon sign in the window. The man he had spoken to the day Muriel Watkins flew through the door was behind the cash register.

"Good morning. Do you remember me?" Jim asked.

The man was middle-aged, with a looming forehead and thinning hair. He seemed supremely uninterested in Jim. "Vaguely. Remind me."

"One of your regulars, Muriel Watkins, almost leveled me in front of your shop not long ago. You came out to check if I was okay, which I appreciated."

The man brightened. "Now I remember. I hope you're not here to tell me you're suing my shop."

"Not at all. I came back to see if you could answer a few questions."

The man gestured to the rear where Jim and he could talk without being overheard by the women waiting their turn.

"Go ahead with your questions." The man sounded curious, not apprehensive.

Jim explained who he was, why he was involved. "Have you ever heard Muriel Watkins threaten anybody, physically threaten?"

"You mean, I'll kill you, you motherfucker? Like that?"

"Not necessarily those precise words, but yes, like that."

"All the time. She has a permanent grudge against humanity."

"I heard you tell her never to come back, but I take it she still does."

The man shrugged. "I need the business. Do you have any idea how many beauty shops there are on this street?"

"Actually, I do," Jim replied.

"Most of my customers are regulars. They're used to Muriel. They laugh off her threats and insults, which makes her furious. Sometimes she goes too far and I ban her from the shop. Muriel always pleads with me to take her back, and I always relent. As obnoxious as she is, she's part of Rosie's."

"You've never worried she might carry out a threat?"

"At first I did. When her tirades started I warned her, I'll call the cops unless you keep it civil."

"Did she stop?"

"Not entirely, but she cooled it. Then the regulars caught on and started teasing her instead of taking her seriously. Muriel's lonely, she needs company as much as you or me. I can't bring myself to hate her. Do you think she had something to do with the bus driver's murder? Is that what you're saying? What about the guy who's behind bars, you don't think he did it?"

"I do not. I witnessed the shooting and the guy behind bars was not the man I saw pull the trigger."

A customer entered the shop and took a seat.

"I have to get back to work." The man held out his hand. "Alonso Sosa."

Jim shook it. "Jim Randall." Jim left the shop and headed towards The Long Gone. Having been inside Rosie's, he now felt like a citizen of Beauty Shop Row instead of a tourist. What had he learned about Muriel Watkins? That she was a hothead, a thorn in everyone's side, but a person somehow involved in a murder? Based on what Jim had learned about her, she now seemed the proverbial lonely person, a disgruntled needy person who acted out her loneliness with insults and threats, not deeds. He almost felt sorry for her. Could a person the regulars at Rosie's teased be behind a murder? The theory felt far-fetched now, the conjecture of a man inexperienced at the detective game.

There were empty tables at The Long Gone, a rare sight. Jim took his coffee to a table along the wall where he could see out the window. The coffee was scalding hot. Waiting for it to cool, he moped. Jim was an amateur sleuth, but a pro at moping.

His phone pinged. A text from Ted.

> How are you holding up?

> Fine. Why do you ask?

> Because I've known you for many years and about now is when your resolve usually collapses. Want to grab a quick bite at lunch?

If you promise to keep your
gloating to a minimum.

No gloating, no moping.
A gloat-free, mope-free lunch.
Deal?

They met at a deli across the street from The Long
Gone. The woman who showed them to a table seemed to
resent having customers. Ted looked haggard.

"Are *you* okay?" Jim asked.

"Yes. Why do you ask?"

"Because you look like hell."

Ted rolled his eyes. "A case I'm working has caught me
in a political battle between the governor and the speaker
of the house. I *hate* this part of my job, I just want to do
law."

"I don't know how you stand it."

"My boss absorbs most of the political flak, thank God.
Where is the damn waitress? I don't have all day."

When she appeared, Ted ordered a tuna salad
sandwich, Jim a bowl of lentil soap.

"That's all you're having?" Ted asked.

"This is how I keep my waistline."

Ted guffawed. "Ha!"

"Only one guffaw?" Jim challenged.

"For now. That's all I've got in me now. Seriously, Jim,
are you holding a grudge against me because of the Benoit
verdict?"

"A grudge? Never. In fact, I'm questioning myself. How about you? Any second thoughts about Benoit?" It was a throwaway line, not a serious question. Ted's long silence in response startled Jim.

"Wait. Don't tell me. You're having second thoughts?"

"Cone of silence?"

Jim nodded. "Always."

Ted started to speak but was interrupted by a young man bringing Jim's soup. "Enjoy," he brightly said.

Jim grumbled when the young man left. "Enjoy. How does everything taste so far? I haven't tried it yet. So how does everything look?"

"Now, now, he's just doing his job."

Jim tried his soup. "Actually, it's not bad. What were you saying?"

Ted explained. "When we first questioned Benoit, he claimed to be getting high with a friend at the time of Ricardo Abbé's murder. We followed up with the friend, who refused to confirm it, so we discounted Benoit's alibi. That was one of the factors that caused us to charge Benoit with murder."

"I think I know where this is heading," Jim said.

"The friend stepped forward last week, said he had been afraid to get in trouble if he told the truth. The friend now confirms Benoit's alibi."

"Which puts you in a political and legal bind. What are you going to do?"

"There was plenty of evidence against Benoit in addition to the lack of an alibi, so I'm not inclined to reopen the case, which makes the governor exceedingly happy because he's up for reelection and wants Benoit to stay behind bars. Which makes me think I'm selling out by not reopening the case."

"I don't envy you, Ted."

"You've told me you think Benoit is innocent, so you should be glad."

"I'm less sure about who is guilty than I was."

"You're a big help."

They shook hands outside the deli.

"I don't know how much longer I want to stay in this job, Jim."

"Don't say that, you're too valuable to the DA's office."

"You retired. Maybe it's my turn."

"Don't do anything rash. You love your job."

"But it's wearing me down."

It was a short walk home. Jim's phone rang as he was unlocking his door. He thought it was probably Ted, telling Jim to disregard his gloom and doom.

"Hi, Ted."

"Jim, it's Sasha Cohen."

"Sorry, Sasha. I just left Ted Conover. Thought it was him."

"No problem. Got a minute?"

"I'm about to walk into my house. Hold on."

"Want me to call you back?"

"No, just give me a second. Okay, I'm inside."

"There are rumors floating around that Francois Benoit's murder case may be reopened. Is that why you were talking to Ted Conover?"

"Sasha, you know I'm not going to comment on that."

"So there's some truth to the rumor."

"Whoa, that's not what I said."

"Rest easy, Jim. I won't print conjecture, but neither will it stop me from following up on the rumor."

"I would expect nothing less, Sasha, but don't get ahead of the reality."

"I might be wasting my time, you're saying."

"I'm saying a good reporter like you of course will follow leads but won't go overboard."

With phone still to his ear, Jim sat down in his most comfortable chair. He could feel the muscles of his legs relax. "Anything else?" he asked Sasha.

"No, you've been helpful. I always feel wiser after talking to you."

"I hope you're kidding."

"Bye, Jim."

Phone in hand, sprawled in his favorite chair, having just talked to someone he liked and respected, Jim felt good about the world. Can't have too much of that, he cautioned, so he hauled himself out of his chair and went into his kitchen. His mind was churning, with what he wasn't sure. Reason backwards, his mind was telling him. Get past the shock, focus on what you saw. Start with the bullets going into Ricardo Abbé's head. See the trigger being pulled by a young man with trembling lips, a young man who resembled Tim Watkins. The realization had teetered on the edge of Jim's consciousness until now when the weight of accumulated evidence pushed it over the edge into the spotlight. Think, Jim. What do you know about Tim Watkins? Super-shy teens live mostly in their own worlds and are reluctant to leave them. What or who could coax, cajole, or force a super-shy Tim Watkins out of his world and turn him into a killer? It didn't take a genius to answer that: Muriel Watkins, Tim's mother.

He made coffee and settled down with the newspaper. Considerable time went by when Jim didn't think about anything except what he was reading. Then he noticed his legs. They were jiggling. How long had they been doing that? He was not a nervous-leg man, his nerves usually showed in a growling of his voice, not in jiggling legs, so it startled him. Finally he could sit and read no longer and bolted from the table and out the front door, donning his autumn jacket on the way.

From the sidewalk in front of his house Jim could see the bus stop on the corner. The bus to Lechmere was approaching. Jim ran to catch it. He made it, but once on board vowed never to run again. That was it for a lifetime. Out of breath, he searched for a seat.

A woman not much younger than Jim took pity and offered him her seat.

"Thank you," Jim said, accepting her offer with relief and chagrin.

Jim hardly noticed the myriad shops on Beauty Shop Row. The mystery of how there could be so many shops devoted to beauty did not capture his attention today. He was on a mission.

He got off the bus at East Canton Street and walked up the block to 49 B. He rang the bell. Muriel Watkins opened it immediately.

"What do *you* want?"

"May I come in?"

"Why?"

"We need to talk. Is your son at home?"

"Tim's at school."

"Did he tell you I saw him outside school the other day?"

"Yes, he did."

"He interests me. What are his plans after graduation?"

"Why do you want to know?"

"I like him. He seems like a nice young man, but unsure of himself."

The sourpuss firebrand beamed with pride, which she tried to hide with a frown. "Tim wants to join the Marines."

"Good for him. You must be proud."

She stepped aside. "Come on in. I guess it's all right for a minute."

She led him into the living room, a small square room with a sofa that looked as if it had outlived many slipcovers. "Sit," she commanded, a sourpuss again.

Jim chose a chair rather than the sofa. "I won't stay long."

Muriel was back in character but her fire seemed subdued. "Damn right you won't. No more bullshit, why are you here? What do you want?"

"As your son may have told you, I've been watching him," Jim said.

"Yes, and I want to know why."

"I think you know."

"I have no idea."

"I think you do."

Muriel briefly flared. "Okay, I know what you're doing, and you're wasting your time."

"Oh, I don't think I am. I'm a patient man and eventually you or Tim will tell me what I want to know."

"Don't hold your breath."

"I notice I'm in your house. You must at least be curious."

"I wanted to see what you're up to. It won't happen again."

"Did you know that the key witness in the Benoit trial has recanted his testimony? He now acknowledges he was getting high with Benoit on Cambridge Common at the time of the murder. That gives Benoit an alibi."

"So?"

"The DA will not allow Ricardo Abbé's murder to go unpunished. If Benoit is exonerated, the DA will go after the killer with redoubled effort, I guarantee you."

Muriel tensed as if she were about to spring from her chair. "You have no right to come in my house and accuse me and my son of murder."

"I didn't accuse either of you of anything. You must have a guilty conscience."

"Not at all. Tim and I have nothing to hide."

"Good. Then you won't have to worry when the police come to your door."

She glared at Jim. "I start to like you, then I come to my senses. You're like all the others."

"Others?"

"Who look down on people like me, who don't give me credit for raising a boy who respects his elders, who obeys his mother, unlike so many kids today. I know more about life as it's lived by real people than you and your kind ever will."

"That may be true. Educate me. Tell me about your life."

She seemed to welcome the chance to talk about herself. "My father was a wildcatter in the Oklahoma oil fields. I never knew him, he left Mom when she got pregnant, but Mom and I managed. I dropped out of high school in sophomore year when I had Tim. Nothing has ever been handed to me."

"What about Tim's father?"

Muriel snorted. "I'm surprised he stayed with me long enough to get me pregnant."

"Your young life sounds much like your mother's."

"I suppose."

"You must have a low opinion of men."

"Men aren't worthy of my opinion."

"That bad, huh?"

She shifted in her chair. "I don't like it when you're sympathetic. Scares me."

"Why? Guilty conscience?"

She rose from her chair. "That's enough. I think you should go."

"Whatever you say." Jim rose and headed for the door. The door opened before Jim could reach it, and Tim entered. He looked startled to see Jim in the house.

Jim explained, "Your mom has just told me about her life."

Tim looked puzzled. "Mom?"

Muriel said, "Don't worry, Tim. The judge and I were just having a friendly chat."

"You're not in trouble?"

"No. No trouble."

"Tim, you and I should talk someday," Jim said.

"Why?"

"It could help clear the air."

"Forget it. Bad idea. I have nothing to say to you, now or later."

"Very well. I'll say goodbye for now. Thank you for inviting me into your home," he said to Muriel. Then to Tim, "See you in the schoolyard."

The fresh air felt good. Jim walked aimlessly, his mind more cluttered than clear. Had he made progress? He couldn't say. Tim was rattled to see Jim in his home, that was for sure, but was that progress?

*

Sasha Cohen's long article on the aftermath of Ricardo Abbé's murder was the cover story in the Sunday *Globe* Magazine. Based on public records and interviews with sources, it ended with the question: was the right man in jail for the crime?

Jim read the article twice, the second time to see if Sasha had used anything he had told her in confidence. She had so artfully disguised her sources he couldn't tell. Good for Sasha.

He texted her:

Good article.

You're not angry?

Why would I be?

I used some of what
you told me

Relax, Sasha, you're skillful
at disguising sources

Anything new on a Benoit
retrial?

LOL, if LOL means what I
think it means

I'm impressed. Next for Judge
Randall – emojis

Never. No way.
Not on your life

Jim wanted to know Ted's reaction to the article, so he called Ted after he got off the line with Sasha. "Have you read Sasha Cohen's piece in the *Globe*?"

"Yes."

"You don't sound happy."

"I'm quietly pissed. She made the DA's office look closed-minded. How much did you tell her?"

"Nothing you told me in confidence, Ted."

"I know you wouldn't leak deliberately, but you are taking this case more personally than normal for you and zeal can make even an honorable man slip up."

"Can you hang on a second."

He covered the phone and suggested to Pat that they invite Ted over for dinner.

"To make amends?" she asked.

"I didn't do anything that needs amend-making, but I want Ted to gauge my guilt or innocence for himself."

"I like Ted. Go ahead."

"Thanks for holding, Ted. Pat and I would like to invite you to dinner."

"Bribery, huh?"

"I don't violate confidences, but I do bribe. Pat says to expect leftovers."

*

Ted had never married and presently didn't have a significant other, so he came alone, carrying a bottle of red wine.

Jim checked the label. "This is good stuff. I thought you were pissed about the article."

"Pissed but polite."

The three of them sat in the living room at first, sipping wine and talking shop. By the time they arrayed themselves around Pat's dinner table, the wine was almost gone.

"You two are missed at the courthouse," Ted said. "Your replacements are good but green."

"Everybody's green compared to us," Jim answered. "We're relics."

"Help me out, relics. The *Globe Magazine* article is going to increase the pressure on my office to reopen the Benoit case. How often did you two reopen a case when you were on the bench?"

Pat replied first. "I was reluctant to reopen cases based on one witness changing his or her testimony. Who's to say the witness is telling the truth the second time if they lied the first time?"

"Jim?"

"I would hold a hearing in my chambers to assess the credibility of the witness, then decide."

"What if you conclude the alibi witness is telling the truth this time, but after weighing the totality of evidence against the defendant, you can't justify reopening the case?"

"Then I'd shut it down."

Pat nodded. "Me too."

Jim rose from the table. "Be right back."

"Where are you going?" Pat asked.

"To get more wine."

When Jim returned to the table, Ted and Pat were talking about favorite vacation spots (Pat -Venice; Ted - Key West), and the discussion never returned to the Benoit case.

As Jim and Pat read in bed that night, Jim wanted to know what Pat thought of the evening.

"Given how sensitive feelings were, I was impressed with how smoothly the conversation went," she said.

"What's your guess? Will Ted reopen the case?"

"No idea, and if I knew, I wouldn't tell you. You'd leak."

"Low blow."

"I'm kidding, as you well know."

"I do?"

She kissed him on the cheek. "Yes, you do. Go to sleep."

10

Beauty Shop Row called to Jim, more urgently than ever. He was sure the telltale clue would pop up or out of one of the beauty salons; he hoped it was Rosie's. Alonso Sosa didn't know what Jim was talking about.

"Are you hearing anything new, is what I'm asking."

"Nothing new. We recycle our gossip," Sosa said.

"Has Muriel Watkins been in recently?"

"Not since you were here. Don't know where she's been. She's overdue for a touch up."

Rosie's was full. The snap of scissors, the hum of hair dryers. Women awaiting their turn.

"Hey," Sosa said, "I heard Benoit might get out of prison. Is that true?"

"He might get a retrial. But get out? I wouldn't bet on it."

"Wow! Wouldn't that be something? That's all anyone here is talking about."

"It definitely would be something."

"Wow. Good stuff."

Jim gave Sosa his card. "If you hear anything new, can you let me know?"

"Will do. Want a trim? I do men's hair for special friends."

"Thanks, but I don't have much hair to trim."

"Look your best with what you have, I always say."

Jim headed for the door, but on the way a woman getting a manicure spoke to him. "Muriel Watkins? You're asking about Muriel?"

Jim stopped. "Yes, I am. Do you know her?"

The woman was in her forties and had more hair than she needed. A pair of reading glasses hung by a chain around her neck.

"Do I know her?" The woman and the manicurist exchanged knowing glances. "Betty, do I know Muriel Watkins?"

The manicurist nodded solemnly. "Yes, you do, Cindy."

Cindy spoke to Jim. "We all know Muriel. She's notorious."

"Care to tell me why?"

"I can only speak for myself, but her boy attacked my boy for nothing and when I went to her house to complain, Muriel acted crazy. I asked Bob – Bob's my husband – to straighten her out, but he's afraid to go near her."

"Muriel's son, Tim, physically attacked your son?"

"You don't believe me?"

"I've met Tim and he seems like the last person on earth who would lay a finger on another person," Jim said.

"Normally, yes, but not when he's under his mother's spell."

"How do you know that's what happened here?"

"Muriel feels insulted by life. She's always itching for a fight. She tells Tim she's been insulted, and Tim does the rest."

"Does this happen often?"

"Not often, Tim's able to talk her off her cliff most of the time. But it happens."

The manicurist finished with Cindy's right hand and switched to the left. Jim took advantage of the switch to ask the manicurist a question. "May I ask, do you do Muriel Watkins's nails?"

"I've tried, but she bites her nails something awful. I told her I couldn't help her."

"How did she take that?"

"She went ballistic. Scared me half to death. When she threatened to boycott Rosie's, I prayed to God she would."

"Thank you both very much. I'm Judge Randall, here's my card if you think of anything else." He started to leave.

Betty offered a free manicure. "Looks like you could use one, Judge, if you don't mind my saying."

Jim smiled. "It's hopeless, but thanks."

The hints and clues he had collected started to jell in his mind as soon as he stepped out of Rosie's. Memo to self: walk the Row when your brain needs a boost. All the clues he needed were in his head but had yet to settle down. At the moment, they were constantly changing and rearranging. When they settled into discernable patterns, Muriel Watkins would be the ur-clue and her cowed but obedient son, Tim, would be clue #2. Jim would bet on it.

What if he were wrong? So far, this was all conjecture based on instinct based on twenty-one years on the bench getting to know the minds of people who do unconscionable things. Professional criminals had relatively straightforward motives – money, power, revenge, a need to be part of a group. Amateur criminals were less predictable – motives were harder to find, and when found, often made no sense except to the criminal.

He didn't notice what he was walking past until he reached the end of Beauty Shop Row, only a few blocks from the courthouse district. Was the closeness of courts and beauty shops a coincidence or a portent? Some courts – including Superior Court, Jim's former court – had recently moved to Woburn, and the tall white courthouse where Jim once worked stood empty.

He was approximately equidistant between his house and Pat's. Go home or to Pat's? He decided on home, then the question became walk or take the #69 bus. He did neither; he sat on a bench in a miniature park and waited for inspiration to strike.

He was still there an hour later. He had no new insights but felt more settled. That was good enough for now. He left the park and caught a bus home.

*

Reading in bed that night, the bedroom dark except for twin reading lights: "I'm missing something," Jim said to the darkness of the ceiling.

Next to him, Pat was barely listening.

"Did you hear me?"

"No."

"I said I'm missing something. What is it?"

Pat closed her book, a history of Tudor England. "You're missing an off switch. Go to sleep, Jim."

"Who haven't I talked to?"

"Go to sleep."

"Not until I figure this out."

Pat fell asleep soon thereafter, but Jim stayed awake, turning over scenarios in his mind. When he finally fell asleep he dreamt of deep sea fishing and scuba diving, neither of which he had ever done nor wished to do. He awoke at first light and found Pat half-awake.

"Are you awake?" he asked her.

"Not really."

"It came to me just before I woke up that I've been focusing on Muriel Watkins and son Timothy, but there is another family member I haven't contacted. Connie, the doctor daughter who lives in California."

Pat struggled awake. "You think she's involved?"

"Not necessarily, but she might be able to tell me something about the family that sheds light."

"You're betting everything on Muriel Watkins as the epicenter of the murder. Isn't that risky?"

"Yes, but I can't shake the feeling that she is the key." He reached for his phone.

"What are you doing?"

"Texting Ernie."

Ernie's reply came almost immediately.

> On my morning jog.
> I'll get the info you want as
> soon as I get home.

What Jim wanted was Connie's contact information. It was complicated by the fact that she had taken her ex-husband's last name when she married and hadn't changed her name back to Watkins when she divorced.

Ernie's answer arrived half an hour later.

> Connie's last name is now
> Benjamin. Connie Watkins
> Benjamin, MD. You can reach
> her through the Epidemiology
> Department at San Mateo
> Hospital.

Jim called Dr. Benjamin from his study. He reached her after a long wait on hold listening to aggravating music. Her voice was professional, her manner brisk.

"Dr. Benjamin, my name is Jim Randall. I'm a retired judge of the Massachusetts Superior Court."

"Why on earth are you calling me?"

"I'm currently investigating the murder of a Massachusetts bus driver. I've spoken to your mother and your brother, and I have a few questions you might be able to answer."

Dr. Benjamin's tone and manner changed abruptly, from curious to cold. "Judge Randall, you have reached me at work. I have a busy practice and can't talk now."

"Can I call you later?"

"Not if it concerns my mother. I have not talked to her in over a decade and that's the way I like it. I want nothing to do with her."

"That's an extreme reaction. May I ask why?"

"If you knew her better, you wouldn't have to ask."

"Are you in touch with your brother?"

"Tim's a sweet guy, but our mother is going to ruin him. If he doesn't leave home as soon as he graduates high school, he's doomed. I wish you luck, Judge Randall, but don't call me again."

"Wait, please don't hang up," but it was too late. The line went dead.

Jim went downstairs and found Pat in the living room.

The living room did not get much light in the morning. Pat was reading the newspaper by the light from a floor lamp. Jim sat down next to her. "I reached the daughter. Lot of good it did. She hasn't spoken to her mother in over a decade and wants nothing to do with her."

"Why?"

"I have no idea. She closed down as soon as she learned why I was calling."

"Are you going to try again?"

"Not unless I find something new. Her reaction was immediate and harsh."

He couldn't get the call out of his mind. He had dealt with a lot of professionals like Dr. Benjamin and admired the calm way most handled their jobs. Dr. Benjamin had sounded every inch the professional at the beginning of the phone call, but became a bitter, spiteful daughter by the end. Maybe Tim could tell him why.

He had seen Tim emerge from the high school often enough that he had a rough idea of when his classes were over for the day. Give it a try, Jim. Sit in the park where you can observe the high school door and hope you get lucky.

He didn't the first day; on the second, he lucked out.

Tim was chatting to a young woman and didn't see Jim at first.

"Hello, Tim. Got a minute?"

"Not really."

"I spoke to your sister."

Tim's demeanor changed instantly. Concern for his sister replaced resentment at being bothered by a pesky ex-judge. Tim told the young woman he'd see her tomorrow and gestured to Jim to follow him out of the stream of students. "Is Connie okay? Has she been hurt?"

"No, nothing like that. I called her hoping she could shed light on why you and your mother are circling the wagons."

"What do you mean?"

"When I ask questions of either of you about Ricardo Abbé, you both react as if you are on trial."

Tim frowned. "What did my sister tell you?"

"Not a lot. Or to be more precise, nothing. I did learn that your sister and your mother are estranged."

Tim looked off to the side. "That's an understatement."

"Care to tell me why?"

"I can't because I don't know. Connie and I have different fathers. Hers died when she was a baby, I never knew mine, plus there's a vast age gap between us. Connie was in medical school when I was in junior high. I love my sister, but we're not close. So I can't tell you why she hates our mother."

"She never confided in you?"

"Never. There's the bus. I've got to run." Tim sprinted to catch it.

The flood of students from the school had slowed. Some of the students lingered in the park, in clusters, in twos, but parents pushing strollers and readers leaving the library with an armful of books had for the most part replaced the high schoolers.

Jim felt a sense of desolation. He regretted ever getting involved with the Watkins family. The more he learned about the family, the more troubled it seemed.

Jim had long marveled at Pat's ability to keep things in perspective. In court she had been unflappable, not allowing the horrific to ruin the positive. Jim needed some of her equanimity. He had a bad feeling about how this case would end. He walked to his townhouse a block away. Pat had left a note on the kitchen table.

"Gone to my apartment. I'll make dinner for us."

He took the T. The light off the Charles dazzled. Glory be to the Longfellow Bridge and the Charles River.

They ate dinner in Pat's kitchen. He thought he recognized the chicken they were eating. "Isn't this the chicken from last week?"

"It's safe, Jim. You won't die."

"Is that a promise?"

"Yes, I promise you won't die from eating last week's chicken."

"But if you're wrong, and I die?"

"As you take your last breath, you can gloat."

"Then I will die in peace."

The compact city garden out Pat's back window was lit by buried lamps, which emitted a warm glow. He thought of the variety of light he had seen that day – the blinding morning light in his kitchen, the dim morning light in his living room, the dazzling light crossing the Charles River, and now the subterranean glow coming from Pat's city garden. All was not dark in the world.

He said to Pat: "I spoke to Connie Watkins Benjamin today, Muriel Watkins' daughter, Timothy's sister. She hasn't talked to her mother in over a decade and likes it that way. Her manner changed from medical professional to angry daughter in an instant when I told her why I was calling. Took me aback, her reaction seemed so extreme. I briefly spoke to her brother afterwards and he couldn't or wouldn't tell me what caused the rift. Said his sister never confides in him because of the age gap."

"Let me get this straight. The daughter hasn't spoken to her mother in over a decade?"

"That's what she said. I can't imagine what her mother did to her."

"Maybe Connie's at fault."

"Maybe, but having had run-ins with Muriel myself, I'm more inclined to blame her."

Jim cleared and washed the dishes. He didn't know how to cook but he was a whiz at washing (and he could talk while he cleaned - he was a proud multitasker at the sink). Pat was working her laptop at the kitchen table. After a few moments, she turned the screen so Jim could see. What Jim saw was a photo of a solemn young woman wearing hospital scrubs.

Pat explained. "I got this picture from her hospital website. Here's what Connie looks like."

Jim studied her picture. "I'm trying to grasp that this put-together young woman is related to Muriel Watkins. They look like they're from different galaxies."

"That's probably why they don't speak to each other – no shared language. Think you could entice them to talk to each other if you offered to serve as translator?"

"Questionable."

"I was joking."

"I know, but I've lost my sense of humor."

"What's wrong, Jim? I've never seen you this morose before. What's happened?"

"Muriel Watkins. Muriel Watkins happened."

"She won't be in your life forever, Jim."

"Are you sure? She feels as indelible as a tattoo."

"Tattoos can be removed."

"Not easily. Not Muriel."

11

The Long Gone was almost full the next morning. Only a few chairs were empty, and they were the equivalent of middle seats on a jumbo jet – no one, including Jim, wanted them. Jim decided to break routine and order his coffee to go, which he drank on a bench at the bus stop.

A disheveled woman wheeling a wire basket full of old clothes – a hoarder on wheels – sat down beside him. She rocked back and forth on the bench while grumbling about the need to protect herself. She turned to Jim, "I don't take the Red Line anymore. Know what I mean? Too many rowdy kids. I was a well-mannered girl when I was young. Don't see that today. I don't know what's wrong with kids today." When Jim only grunted in reply, she turned away and resumed her grumbling.

A Harvard Square bus pulled to the curb and several riders got off. The disheveled woman climbed on, bumping her wire basket up the steps, one step at a time. The driver belatedly dipped his bus to help her.

Jim followed the woman onto the bus. Only when seated did he wonder why; he had no reason at the moment to go to Harvard Square. He sat where he sat the morning of Ricardo Abbé's murder. Maybe Jim's brain was staging a replay to give him a chance to review the crime in slow motion.

The bus passed the city hospital and the rehab hospital and Jim's street, then came to the last stop, Harvard Square.

The woman bumped her basket down the steps of the bus and headed towards the church across from Harvard Yard that housed the homeless at night.

He had followed the rabbit down the rabbit hole without finding Wonderland. What had he expected? He gave up on the woman and walked through the gates into Harvard Yard. Students came and went from the freshman dorms that ringed the Yard. Tourists clustered around John Harvard's statue having their pictures taken touching his shiny boot for good luck. A lone young man with black hair and a furtive look was heading towards Jim. The young man was so absorbed in thought that he didn't notice Jim at first. When he did, the young man spun a 180 and took off in the opposite direction. It was Tim Watkins. Jim followed as fast as he could. Tim stopped when he reached the far gate and waited for Jim. "What do you want? I'm getting tired of you," he said when Jim reached him.

"Running into you now wasn't planned, but we need to talk," Jim said, slightly out of breath.

"We've talked enough. I have nothing more to say."

"Tim, I think you do. With a mother like yours, I understand why you'd do such a terrible thing, but you have a long life ahead of you and you won't be able to live with yourself unless you break free of her."

Tim faltered. He looked on the verge of sobbing. "Leave me alone! Please? Just leave me alone!"

With one or two exceptions, people streaming by didn't spare them a glance.

"I'll go for now, Tim, but I won't give up. You'll see me again."

"Fuck you! When I tell my mother what you're doing, you'll be sorry! You don't know what she's like!"

"Oh, I think I do."

"No way. She's out of her mind!" Tim blushed. "She's going to kill me for saying that, and she might kill you too."

"I can take care of myself, but I'm worried about you. You have a lot of life to live, and I'm sure you don't want it to be governed by your mother's resentments."

As Jim started to go, Tim asked, "Is Connie really okay?"

"As far as I could tell over the phone. She cares about you, that's for sure."

"I miss her."

"Why don't you call her?"

Tim shook his head. "I can't. Mom would go ballistic."

With that, they parted. There was more to say, but Jim thought he had made headway and that was enough for now. Alice had her rabbit, Jim had his disheveled woman.

He called Pat on his way home.

"I just encountered Tim Watkins in Harvard Yard. He seemed shaken when I told him I had talked to his sister."

"You sound different. Are you okay?"

"I'm fine. Newly audacious."

"Did you say newly audacious?"

"You don't believe me?"

"Will I recognize you?"

"I'm me only better."

"You're scaring me, Jim."

"You have nothing to worry about. I've made progress, more than I expected, that's all. Maybe I'm feeling a little smug."

"Smug? Now you're feeling smug? I thought you were feeling audacious."

"Can't it be both? Smugly audacious, perhaps?"

Jim and Pat ate dinner that evening at the narrow bistro at the base of Beacon Hill. Jim's mood had swung full circle, and he was in a playful mood. Not a care in the world.

"What's wrong?" Pat said after they ordered.

"Nothing. Why do you ask?"

"You're happy."

"That's wrong?"

"Usually you do not show it. Usually when you're happy you get grouchier."

"I shall let that pass. I made unexpected headway today in the Abbé murder and nothing you say can upset me. Plus I think Tim's going to do the heavy lifting for me from now on. Hardened killers are immune to guilt, Tim is not a hardened killer. Remember what guilt did to Raskolnikov in *Crime and Punishment*."

"But Tim will face a stiff jail sentence if he confesses."

"Tim may be tried as a juvenile and receive a shorter sentence than he would as an adult. Does he fear a jail sentence more than he fears his mother? That is the question."

Pat let the question hang.

"Does your silence mean you think I'm wasting my time?" Jim asked.

"Not at all. I'm proud of you, but I'm also worried about you. Is the mother a danger?"

"She is, but if I'm right about the murder, an innocent man is in prison. If there's a chance of freeing him, I have to try."

*

Jim had never served on juvenile court so he wasn't up to speed on juvenile law. He spent the afternoon cramming as if for an exam. In his law school days, he would have spent the afternoon in the law library (sometimes he missed the law library) but with so much case law and statutory law online now, he didn't need to leave his house. He was out of the habit of force-feeding the law and by the middle of the afternoon, he was exhausted.

His phone rang. A number he didn't know. As a rule he didn't answer calls from numbers he didn't know because he didn't want to: (a) save money on his electric bill, (b) buy a time-share in Florida, or (c) answer a few questions about a recent purchase. But he answered the phone anyway, welcoming the diversion.

"Hello?"

"Judge Randall?" A woman's voice. Brisk, to the point.

"Yes."

"This is Dr. Connie Benjamin, Tim Watkins' sister. We spoke earlier."

"Good afternoon, Doctor Benjamin. I'm surprised to hear from you again."

"Your call touched my conscience, hardened though it is. As much as I despise my mother, she is still my mother and I'd like to know how she is doing. I want nothing to do with her, but how is she doing?"

"I first met your mother when she flew out the door of a beauty salon and almost knocked me over. That was the high point of our acquaintance. It's been downhill from there."

"Let me guess. She didn't apologize, she yelled at you for being in her way."

"Correct."

"Okay, I understand better now. Can you at least tell me how she looks? She used to take great care of her appearance."

"Her appearance is as unruly as her temper. I see a woman who is consumed by grievances, real and imagined."

"How is my brother? Have you met him?"

"Yes. He seems physically fine but is under considerable pressure from your mother."

"I still don't understand why you contacted me. You haven't adequately explained."

"I'll be glad to." Go for it, he urged himself. Don't hold back, be your newly audacious self. "This will come as a shock, Dr. Benjamin, but I have reason to believe that your mother may be responsible for the murder of an MBTA bus driver, and I suspect, but with less certainty, that your brother was the killer."

The phone went dead. Jim called back. There was no answer.

The view out Jim's back window hadn't changed – same trees, same roof tops – yet Jim's intuition that his investigation had entered the home stretch had hardened into certainty.

He checked his watch. The high school was about to let out for the day. If he hurried, he might catch Tim before he got on the bus home.

Jim hurried to the stop in front of the school. The usual scrum of students waited to get on the Lechmere bus. Three boys started pushing and punching each other; it was harmless but to someone who didn't know teenagers, it looked real. It continued until one of the guys bumped into a young girl, causing her to drop her books and call the boys creeps and worse. The boys giggled and shoved onto the bus. In the bustle, Jim almost missed seeing Watkins join the scrum. "Tim!" Jim called.

Tim turned to look. When he saw who was calling him, he shook his head and double-timed onto the bus. Jim followed as quickly as he could and took a seat several rows behind Tim.

The bus passed The Long Gone and the first of the salons on Beauty Shop Row. Wouldn't it be ironic if Muriel careened out the door of Rosie's House Of Beauty just as her son passed in the Lechmere bus? But the bus passed by Rosie's without incident.

As the bus approached East Canton Street a stop later, Tim bolted from his seat and was out the door the moment the door opened, forcing Jim to hurry if he wanted to tail him.

No need to hurry. Tim was waiting for him on the curb.

"You're in trouble, Judge. I told my mother you're stalking me."

"And so far I'm still in one piece. Imagine that."

"I'm warning you, she has a gun. She got it when Dad left her, and she's crazy enough to use it. Got to go, Mom will wonder where I am."

"I spoke to your sister again."

Tim froze. "You spoke to Connie again?"

"Yes."

"What did she say?"

"She wanted to know how you are doing."

"Did you tell her I miss her?"

"I didn't have time. She hung up on me."

Tim turned towards his house. "I'm asking you politely to leave Mom and me alone. I won't be polite next time."

"Tim, I wish I could. If I'm right about what your mom made you do, an innocent man is in prison and I can't let that pass."

They were standing on the corner of East Canton Street. Jim could see Tim's yellow house up the street.

"I don't hate you, Judge, but if you don't leave me alone I can't promise you won't be hurt."

"I can't drop this, Tim, I'm sorry. If you confess, given your age and the extenuating circumstances of your volatile mother, I think you could get out of prison while you've still got a life."

"What about Mom? What would happen to her?"

"The Assistant DA is a friend of mine. I'll talk to him and explain the circumstances. Your mother will be incarcerated, but for how long and in what kind of facility will depend on how cooperative you and she are."

Jim watched as Tim considered his offer. What must be going through his head? What was it like for a quiet, self-effacing young man to have a maniacal mother like Muriel?

"I'm sorry, Judge. Crazy or sane, she is my mother, and I can't turn her in."

Tim walked away and didn't look back until he reached his house, when he briefly glanced in Jim's direction. The front door opened a crack and Muriel's face appeared. From that distance, Muriel Watkins looked benign.

12

Ted was wary about meeting Jim for dinner.

"Is there an agenda?"

"To catch up. To keep in touch."

He could hear Ted smile. "No lectures? No sermons?"

"I can do those too, if you want."

"There's a new dive I've been meaning to try, Harlow's Hash House. It's gotten good reviews from people in my office."

The restaurant was in a close-knit neighborhood soon to be gentrified if recent East Cambridge history was any indication. The restaurant reeked of faux-maleness. In general, Jim hated faux-anything, but he didn't mind the faux-maleness of Harlow's Hash House because it was so over the top.

"I'll let you choose the wine," Ted said.

"Will you pay for it?"

"Not on your life."

"Then I'll go for the cheap stuff."

Jim ordered a bottle of a standard Côtes du Rhône. Serviceable yet ordinary, bland yet inoffensive. "Ted, I think I'm close to solving the Abbé murder to your satisfaction as well as mine."

"Want to let me in on it?"

"Not yet. You're going to need an open mind."

"Which you sometimes think I don't have."

"Which you sometimes don't, but you are persuadable, which redeems you."

Jim liked the food better than the wine, which was unusual for him. Neither Ted nor Jim spoke as they dug in.

"Not bad," Jim said.

"I like it," replied Ted.

"I can tell you this much. Tim Watkins is a very unlucky young man to have a mother like Muriel. I have tapped into a very dysfunctional family and Muriel is the mother lode, so to speak."

"I have no idea what you just said."

"All shall become clear. What about you? Any cracks in your certainty that the right man is in prison?"

"None. I think Benoit confessed without full awareness of what he was doing and then regretted it when he found himself in prison for the rest of his life, but I believe his confession. Why are you looking at me that way?"

"What way?"

"Like I'm a stranger."

"I'm trying to adjust to seeing you not as a friend or as a lawyer arguing a case in my courtroom, but as the man who stands in the way of an innocent man being freed from prison."

"We don't have to fight over this. Present me with evidence and I'll reopen the case."

Jim raised his wine glass. "You're on."

Pat was reading in the living room when Jim got home. "How was dinner?" she asked.

"Fine. We had a good time."

"A good time?"

"Yes, I like Ted."

"As I know, but I also know you like to be right."

"I think I can convince him. And the food was surprisingly good."

"Did you have the hash?"

"No, I had chicken piccata."

"You remember what you ate? I'm stunned."

"Don't make fun of me. What did you do for dinner?"

"I grazed. A little of this, a little of that."

Jim sat in the easy chair next to Pat. Her profile was that of a formidable woman. If anyone could take her lightly, he'd like to meet them.

"Muriel Watkins knows I'm leaning on her son. I'm counting on a reaction from her or him one of these days."

"Don't take foolish risks, Jim. For a sober-minded man, you have a reckless side."

"You mean an audacious side. Don't worry. I'm especially aware of risk now that I know she has a gun."

Pat looked horrified. "She has a gun?"

"Yes, Tim told me."

"I'm very mad at you, Jim. If she has a gun and she is as unhinged as you say, you could be in great danger."

"Don't worry, I'm being cautious."

"How can you be audacious and cautious at the same time?"

"Dexterity. I am dexterous."

"Jim, you may not realize this, but this investigation has tied you in knots. I've seen it happen before. This is when you make mistakes."

"I promise I'll be careful. Now I'm going upstairs to my study to feel wise." He climbed the stairs to the third floor, which he could still do without getting winded. His legs felt tired by the end, but he didn't get winded. If Muriel Watkins chased him, she'd probably catch him, but he wouldn't be winded when she did.

As he had quipped to Pat, he felt wise in his study. Occasionally he had felt wise on the judge's bench, but he felt wisest alone in his study. How could he not, surrounded as he was by Cicero and Plato and with no one around to contradict him?

Did he have the right to meddle with a jury verdict? Benoit had a lengthy rap sheet before his conviction for murder. Tim Watkins had a clean record. Free Benoit and put Tim Watkins in prison? Benoit had received a fair trial and been found guilty by a jury of his peers. How could Jim, who believed in juries, who had devoted his life to the rule of law, be justified in overturning a jury verdict?

Light reading, that's what Jim needed. Something to take his mind off the choice he faced. Life was best when taken tongue-in-cheek and ego-in-check. He picked a Maigret mystery off his shelf and settled down to read. Georges Simenon had written some seventy-five Inspector Maigrets, and Jim had read at least half of them. There were times he started to read one and thirty pages in realized he had read it before. No matter, he still enjoyed them and didn't really care if he already knew whodunnit. The pleasure was in watching Maigret solve crimes in his unorthodox way.

There was one big difference between Jim and Inspector Maigret: Maigret knew what he was doing, Judge Randall tried his best and hoped it was good enough. How could it be otherwise? Maigret was a pro, Jim an amateur. On the other hand, even a pro like Inspector Maigret lost heart midway through every case. At such times, Maigret's colleagues knew to stay out of his way and let him brood. In Maigret's hands, brooding was an effective crime-solving technique. Jim, too, brooded midway through most investigations, but for him, brooding was less a crime-solving tool than a way to stall for time.

Jim went to his study window. It had gotten dark, but there was still enough of a glow on the horizon to illuminate the angular rooftops of Mid-Cambridge. Geometry students could learn a lot from the view out Jim's window.

Jim believed his ego was in check, but realized that the years of being called "Your Honor" had spoiled him. What if he were in more danger than he realized? Muriel Watkins certainly was eccentric, but personally dangerous? He didn't think so, nor did he think she could coerce Tim into doing her dirty work a second time. And what if he were entirely wrong about Muriel and she had not bullied Tim into killing Ricardo Abbé? He hated to admit that Ted could be right and that the murder had nothing to do with Muriel. Face it, Jim, in spite of your efforts to think of yourself as uninfected by the American-male disease of hyper-competitiveness, you hate to lose. Even to a friend like Ted, *especially* to a friend like Ted.

Get thee downstairs, Jim, and sit with Pat until you are over your brooding self. She had been right, he *was* tying himself into knots.

A restless night. A grumpy morning.

"You leave something to be desired as a companion this morning," Pat said over coffee.

Jim tried being lighthearted: "To the contrary, I believe I am making the ultimate sacrifice by having my coffee at home."

"But you'll go to The Long Gone as soon as I leave."

"Maybe. What of it?"

Pat went to Back Bay in late morning to meet a friend for lunch. Jim did not go to The Long Gone after she left. He'd gloat to her that evening. His homebound lunch consisted of leftover meatloaf. He barely noticed what he was eating.

After lunch he settled down to read his current Maigret – *Maigret Gets Angry*. After a chapter or two he found his mind wandering. Instead of wondering how Maigret would solve his case, he found himself wondering how he, Jim, was going to prove that Muriel Watkins was the catalyst in the murder of Ricardo Abbé. The ringing of the doorbell came as a welcome interruption. He lifted himself out of his chair and went to the front door. When he opened it, he found himself face-to-face with none other than Muriel Watkins and her son Tim. Muriel looked angry, Tim looked sheepish.

Caught off guard, Jim mumbled, "Good afternoon."

"My son has something to tell you." Muriel nudged her son. "Go on, Timothy, tell him what you told me."

Tim lowered his eyes as he spoke. "I told Mom you were following me. I told her that I want you to leave me alone."

"You hear that, Judge? My son wants you to leave him alone."

"I think you misunderstood him. I think he wants you to leave him alone."

"Do you hear what he's trying to do, Tim? Do you? He's trying to turn you against me. Your mother, the woman who raised you, stood by you, encouraged you when no one else would."

Tim's face grew red. "Do you think I don't know what he's doing, Mom? Do you think I'm dumb? I love you but get off my back. Haven't you done enough damage?"

"That's good, Tim. Speak for yourself," Jim said.

Tim would have none of that. He glared at Jim. "You too, Judge Randall. Back off! I don't need your help anymore. Leave mom and me alone."

Jim was about to answer, but Muriel interrupted. "Good, Tim. Let's go home, son. I think the Judge gets our point." Muriel took Tim by the arm and pulled him away.

Jim watched them cross the street to the bus stop on the corner. They didn't have long to wait. A Lechmere bus swooped to a stop and mother, son, and the ghost of Ricardo Abbé climbed aboard.

*

Jim and Pat ate dinner that night at the narrow bistro at the base of Beacon Hill. While waiting for the wine to come, Jim said, "I'll finish telling you about Tim and Muriel Watkins's house call."

Jim had already given Pat the Cliff Notes version. Now he filled in the details.

"If I read Tim correctly, he feels humiliated by the stranglehold his mother has on him. I think he's ready to break with her."

"By confessing to murder?"

"I think he's close to confessing, even though he knows that confessing will send him to prison. Humiliation can be more painful than prison. I think Tim knows that he has to break free of his mother if he wants to rid himself of the humiliation he feels. In doing so, he'll also free Francois Benoit. I like Tim. I think he'll do the right thing."

"Go back to the beginning. I still don't understand why Muriel Watkins would want Ricardo Abbé dead."

"Neither do I. That's the missing piece."

"A fairly large piece, don't you think?"

"Too big a missing piece if I were in Ted's prosecutorial shoes, but I'm not. I'm a gumshoe."

"Be careful, Jim. All joking aside, you'll do real damage to yourself and others if you're wrong. By the way, did Muriel show her gun at your house?"

Jim scoffed. "No, she didn't show her gun, that's melodramatic."

"From your descriptions of her, I'd say that she is melodrama personified."

"Crazy is more like it."

A young waitperson appeared and chirped, "Dessert?"

They had espresso but skipped dessert and walked uphill to Pat's after they left the bistro The streets at the top of Beacon Hill seemed silent by comparison to those at the base of the hill.

It was a nice night. Clear skies, dry air. "Seriously, Jim," Pat said, breaking the nighttime quiet. "Could you be doing more harm than good?"

"I've considered that, but I don't think so."

"What if he didn't do anything?"

"Tim?"

"Yes, the son. What if you're right and the mother is a monster. She wouldn't be the first monster mother in history, but most don't make their sons murder a bus driver."

They reached Pat's apartment. She had drawn the translucent curtains and left a living room light on while they were at dinner. From the sidewalk, her windows glowed softly.

She fumbled with the key. "I'm getting arthritis."

"Need help?"

"Nope." She turned the key and the door opened wide.

13

Nearing seventy, Jim took stock of his health. He didn't smoke and while he liked wine, he didn't abuse it. He could stand to lose a few pounds, but compared to a lot of men his age, he was in good shape. He liked to walk, but he didn't strive for distance or keep a tally.

What he should do is get more exercise when he was at his house in Vermont. He loved the Vermont countryside and the air was invigorating. If he got in the habit there, he felt confident that would function as an on-ramp to regular exercise in Cambridge. Two problems with that scenario: it presupposed frequent enough stays in Vermont to establish a routine and it assumed he would keep up the routine when he returned home, which was not a given. Will power about mental work he had, but not about exercise.

He had these thoughts the next morning on his walk to The Long Gone. It was still lightweight jacket weather, but down coats would soon muscle windbreakers aside. The weather is chill, The Long Gone is full, he chanted to himself as he took his dark roast to one of the few empty seats.

The couple on his right was planning a birthday party for a friend they apparently didn't like very much. The couple on his left was texting each other and trading giggles. A young man sitting by himself was highlighting passages in a contracts case book.

Jim's phone pinged. A text from Dr. Connie Watkins Benjamin.

> In town unexpectedly for a
> medical conference.
> Can we meet?

Jim texted back.

> Where are you staying?

> The Marriott near MIT

They met in the hotel lobby. Dr. Connie Benjamin in person was high-intensity. She spoke quickly but clearly, each word distinct. He could imagine her in scrubs, barking orders to interns.

They shook hands. "I didn't expect we'd ever meet in person," Jim said.

"Me either. I signed up for this conference at the last minute because I thought to myself, why should Tim have to bear our mother alone? He shouldn't, so I'm here."

"How long are you in town?"

"The conference lasts three days. Depending how things go with Tim and my mom, I may stay a day or two longer."

"Do your mother and Tim know you are here?"

"My mother, no. Tim, yes. I called him before I left San Mateo. We always got along, but the age gap was so wide that we were never close. He was very surprised to hear from me. Let me ask you the salient question. Do you honestly believe my mother coerced Tim into killing the bus driver?"

"Yes, I do. Sorry."

She gave a slight nod. "Knowing my mother, it wouldn't surprise me. Keep in mind that I'm long out of touch, but from what I know of her loose connection with reality, it's certainly plausible."

"Did you tell Tim that?"

"Yes."

"How did he react?"

"He went deathly silent, which is one of the reasons I'm inclined to think he's guilty."

The hotel lobby hummed with the businesslike buzz of a dozen deals. Jim imagined Dr. Benjamin preparing her thoughts for a PowerPoint presentation. He decided he didn't particularly like her but would be delighted to have her for his doctor. When she spoke again, it was with firmness. "I told Tim we needed to settle scores. He agreed to meet me today after school. I told him you'd be with me."

"He didn't object to that?"

"He did not. I think he wants this to be over. Well?"

"Of course. And thanks."

They met at the same pizza parlor where – at the beginning of his investigation – Jim had asked the high school students if any of them knew anything about the murder. Jim figured Tim would be more at ease in a student hangout.

Dr. Benjamin and Jim got there first. Tim locked eyes with his sister as soon as he walked in. He showed no emotion at first, but when he sat down beside her, he teared up. "Hi," he said.

"It's wonderful to see you, Tim. I wouldn't have recognized you."

"Are you kidding? I wouldn't recognize you even if you were wearing a name tag. Actually, I see you are. Okay if I hug you?"

"Oh, you idiot! Come here."

Jim didn't interrupt their hug. He couldn't even if he tried.

Tim spoke first. "Why did you drop out of touch, sis? I didn't understand then and I don't understand now."

"I had my reasons, but first I want to talk about the elephant in the room. The judge and I agree that if you were involved in any way with Mr. Abbé's murder, you need to confess. You were always a sweet kid who was appalled to see anybody get hurt. I can only guess what Mom did to make you do it, but your conscience will destroy you if you keep what you did inside."

Tim threw up his hands. "Et tu, sis?"

"Keep your voice down," Connie admonished.

"Seriously. Why would I want Mr. Abbé dead? He was a nice man,"

"No one is saying you wanted to do it, but you did. You did, didn't you?"

Tim jumped from his chair. "I'm not taking any more of this! It's good to see you, sis, but I've heard enough from you and your...your bodyguard!" He gestured at Jim. "Both of you think Mom is a moral monster, and that I'm a coward and a weakling for giving in to her."

Jim said, "Not a weakling nor a coward. Loving and intimidated, I would say. You love and fear your mother in equal measure. The pressure she put on you must have been unbearable to make you do something so against your nature."

"You don't know the whole story, she's not like that."

"She's not? Could've fooled me."

"She thought she was avenging Connie, don't you see?"

Jim looked at Connie. "No, I don't," he said with some surprise.

"Nor do I," Connie said. "Maybe you should enlighten us, Tim."

Jim didn't let Tim answer. "Not here. Too public. We need privacy. Let's take a walk."

They left the coffee shop together and walked in the direction of Beauty Shop Row.

Tim looked rattled. The closer they got to the Row, the more rattled he looked.

Jim noticed. "What's wrong Tim? You're sweating. Are you sick?"

"Fuck you!"

"Would you rather take a bus, Tim? The Lechmere bus stops on the corner. We could take that."

"No, I would not rather take a bus! I know what you and my sister are doing, and you both can go straight to hell!"

When they reached the bus stop at the beginning of Beauty Shop Row, Tim began hyperventilating.

"Are you okay, Tim? Do you want to sit down?" Jim asked.

"I'm fine, and no! I don't want to sit down."

Jim kept his voice low, his tone neutral. "This is where you got on the bus the morning you shot Ricardo Abbé, isn't it, Tim? This is the corner where you waited, wrestling with your conscience, hearing your mother's voice in your head urging you not to be a wimp."

"I don't remember!"

"You got on the bus and fired two shots point blank into Mr. Abbé's head. That's right, isn't it, Tim? I saw you do it, Tim. Did the shots sound as loud to you as they did to me?"

Tim was on the verge of tears. "You're not going to let up, are you? Either of you."

"Afraid not. It's not in my nature," Jim said.

"And I care too much about you to quit," Connie said. "You have to face what you did, Tim. You have to acknowledge it to yourself. You can't move on until you do."

"If you care so much, sis, why did you leave me alone with Mom when I was too young to defend myself?" Tim's voice was strained. A few passersby turned to look. "I grew up without anyone to protect me from Mom!"

"I'm sorry about that, Tim. I really am. Self-preservation got in the way."

"You need to explain that to me someday. How could you abandon me to Mom when you knew what she was like?"

"To explain why will take time, which I don't have now. I have to go to my conference. Let's meet tomorrow and I'll explain. Okay?"

"You promise? You won't disappear like you did before? You won't run out on me again?"

"I promise." They were almost at East Canton Street. "Are you going to the house now?" Connie asked Tim.

"Yes, I am. Are you coming?"

"Tomorrow, after I try to explain why I failed you. I'll come with you and we'll talk to Mom together." Connie put her hand on Tim's shoulder. "This will get worse before it gets better, Tim. There will be pain, lots of pain, but I'll be in your life from now on. You won't be alone."

*

Jim couldn't fall asleep that night. Pat was beside him, but sleep wouldn't come. He awoke in the morning as tired as when he went to bed.

"I'm meeting Tim and his sister, Connie, at the Marriott in an hour. "

The coffee shop at the Marriott was generic-hotel coffee shop. Jim arrived first and chose a corner booth, Tim arrived next looking scared, Connie entered last. She looked considerably older than the day before.

"I need caffeine," she said before sitting. A waitress wielding a coffee pot passed by the table and Connie almost tackled her. When her cup was full, Connie began her tale.

"Listen closely, Tim, because I'm only going to tell you this once. When I was in high school, I used to ride the #69 bus to school. Mr. Abbé often drove the bus. We used to tease him, and he didn't seem to mind. Once in a while we could tell he even liked it. Anyway, it was fun for us because he seemed so gruff on the outside. He made clear to us that we were not to tease him while he was driving, but when we got on and off, we could tease him all we wanted. And we did. "I remember once when I casually mentioned to Mom that Mr. Abbé liked being teased, and Mom got red in the face. Black people have learned how to hide their true feelings around white people, she told me. Don't be deceived by Mr. Abbé, she said. Don't 'cozy up' to him— those were the exact words she used – don't 'cozy up' to him. My friends laughed when I told them what she said. Mr. Abbé was our favorite bus driver. Never angry at us like some of the drivers. My friends thought Mom was a little eccentric, a little nuts, a little 'off her rocker.' So did I."

Connie paused in her story, and Tim seized the moment to ask, "That was it? Her warnings about Mr. Abbé caused the rift between you and Mom?"

"No, the warnings were just the beginning."

"So tell us the rest of the story."

"Mom imagined Mr. Abbé saying things to me, doing things to me which he never did. Never. He was always a gentleman. But she wouldn't be convinced. Hearing her imagine disgusting things he did to me made me sick. I couldn't believe she was serious, but good God, was she ever! It got so bad that she would meet me at the door when I came home from school and grill me on what Mr. Abbé had done or said to me that day. I couldn't stop her accusations, no matter how hard I tried. You were so young you didn't know what was going on, so you tuned out. A wise thing to do. I wish I could've tuned out, but I couldn't. What I did instead was to do well enough in school to graduate a year early with a full scholarship and never look back. I rarely came home while I was in college, and never in med school. It broke my heart to see what she was doing to you, but I had to protect myself. I'm so sorry, Tim. I look at you now and I'm ashamed of myself."

Tim shook his head in dismay. "I had no idea how hard it was for you. I remember you and Mom screaming at each other but I didn't know why, so I just pretended it wasn't happening."

"You were too young to understand. Don't blame yourself."

"I have to ask…" Embarrassment reddened Tim's face. "Did Mr. Abbé ever touch you?"

"Absolutely not. Never. I told Mom that, but she refused to believe me."

Tim looked stricken. "Mom said he did, and I believed her."

"She told you he touched me?"

"Yes, and worse. She told me Mr. Abbé persuaded you to meet him after school and did things to you she refused to talk about because they were so disgusting."

"That's a lie! That's categorically false! You didn't believe her, did you?"

"I'm ashamed to say I did. She was my mother, as crazy as she was, and when your mother tells you something over and over, you feel disloyal if you don't believe her. The story of what Mr. Abbé did to you became part of my history."

Connie pleaded, "Why didn't you ask me, Tim? Why didn't you ask me if it were true?"

"I didn't know what to do. I was just a kid. What would I do if you said yes, he did those things? Besides, you were never around. You avoided being home as much as you could. In your absence, the story grew and grew in my mind until it became reality."

"I failed you, Tim. I failed you, and I'm really, really sorry. If we had been closer, you would have had a better chance of resisting Mom."

Tim looked at the time. "I've got to get to school. When are you heading back to California, sis?"

"After the conference ends tomorrow."

Tim thought for a moment. "I need to see you tomorrow before you go. It's time for me to clear the air."

*

Jim puttered around his townhouse for the rest of the day. He puttered well. He liked to fill unstructured time by finding connections between ideas. Since there were always random ideas in his mind, there was always something to do. For example, how could a hate-filled person like Muriel Watkins have a daughter like Connie, whose life was devoted to healing? Another, if Tim did carry out his mother's hate-filled wishes, how could he be the shy, decent kid he seemed to be?

Pat arrived for the night in mid-putter. Jim was occupying himself by straightening the book piles on his coffee table. In unsettled times, he liked the corners of his book piles to be perfectly square.

"Hi," Pat said as she walked into the living room. "Straightening up?"

"You should have seen it before. Chaos, utter chaos."

"I saw it. Yesterday. Remember me? I'm your companion, your lover, and your scold." She took off her coat and draped it over the back of a chair. "I want to hear about your meeting with Connie and Tim. Was it productive?"

"I believe so. They're meeting again tomorrow before Connie flies home. I'll know more then."

"I think you should open a bottle of the wine you save for special occasions."

"I don't know if tomorrow will be a special occasion or a major letdown, but I like the idea of opening a good bottle of wine."

He chose a 2012 Pic St. Loup, one of his favorite Languedoc wines. It was good but not good enough to stop his mind from racing. What would he do if Tim didn't confess to his sister tomorrow? What should he, Jim, do if he had reached a dead end? Start over? Quit?

"I've never seen you this preoccupied," Pat said midway through the meal.

"Really?"

"Are you thinking of Muriel Watkins?"

"No, I'm thinking of Connie and Tim. I'm more concerned about them than Muriel at this stage. Everything hinges on what Tim tells Connie when they meet."

Pat muttered, "Everything depends on the red wheelbarrow...."

"What are you talking about?" Jim asked, puzzled.

"It's from a William Carlos Williams poem."

Jim absorbed that for a moment. "You are inscrutable."

Jim heard nothing from Connie or Tim the following day until this from Connie at 4:30 p.m.

> My plane leaves Logan at
> 9:15. Can you meet me at the
> airport before I go?

The quickest way to the airport from Jim's house was via I-93 and the Sumner Tunnel, but the traffic getting to the tunnel could clog badly, so Jim took the Mass Pike and the Ted Williams tunnel, a twenty minute drive when traffic was light, but today it took Jim forty. Connie was flying out of terminal C, currently undergoing major renovation, which had turned the terminal into a construction zone.

He spotted Connie standing near the TSA line.

"Hi," he said, approaching.

"We don't have much time. My plane boards in a few minutes."

"I'll be quick. Did you and Tim meet today?"

"Yes, we did. Ready?"

"Ready."

"Okay, here goes. Tim didn't need encouragement. Without hesitation he confessed that he shot Mr. Abbé. He described the shooting as an out-of-body experience following months and months of intense pressure from Mom to restore the family honor by killing the man who had molested me. Tim said he came to his senses as soon as he pulled the trigger. Horrified by what he had done, he went into deep denial, which is where he stayed until you came along. When you approached him with questions, his defenses began to crumble, and when I came east to see him, what was left of his defenses collapsed. He's ready to go with you to the DA."

"Does he realize that he will serve time and most likely, so will your mother?"

"Yes. Turning Mom in is the hardest part for him. While he can accept that he'll go to prison, turning in his mother seems unforgivable. But he's ready to. He wants to atone for what he did as best he can."

"Are you okay with that?"

"I'm horrified, ashamed, gutted, but I admire Tim for confessing. Mom is a racist, a bigot, and a vicious person, and I'm struggling with the question, is it wrong to love her? I don't think I'll ever answer that question to my satisfaction."

"Does your mother know Tim is going to turn himself in?"

"Yes. We told her today. It was not pretty."

For the first time, Jim became aware of the rolling of suitcases, the bickering of couples, and the admonishments of parents. For a moment he wished he were flying somewhere distant and peaceful, but the only place he really wanted to be – other than anywhere with Pat – was his house in Vermont, which is where he would go as soon as this was over.

Connie continued. "Mom went berserk. Wailing, weeping, 'I can't believe my own son would do this to me,' etc. Total meltdown. I have to give Tim credit. Somewhere in his shy soul, he is a strong young man."

An announcement came over the PA system – "Now boarding, gate 21, flight 33 nonstop to San Francisco."

"That's my flight," Connie said.

"I'll alert Ted Conover to expect a visit from Tim and me. Ted is the Assistant DA and a longtime friend of mine. Tim will get a fair deal."

Connie stood and offered her hand. "It's been a privilege, Judge Randall. Maybe we'll meet again. In the meantime, thank you, thank you for all you've done." She turned and headed for the gate. Jim waited until she was out of sight, then texted Tim.

> At the airport. Just met with Connie. She told me what you said today. With your permission, I will arrange a meeting for you, me, and my friend, Assistant DA Ted Conover. Okay?

Tim replied quickly:

> Do it before I lose my nerve.

14

Ted's office looked as pristine as ever. Same family photos on his desk, same sailboat painting on the wall. If anything had been moved even an inch, Jim couldn't tell.

Jim made the introductions. "Ted, this is Tim Watkins."

They shook hands. "Hello, Tim. I'm ADA Ted Conover. Pleased to meet you. Have a seat.

Tim looked ashamed and proud, defeated and defiant.

Ted began. "I understand you have something to tell me regarding the murder of Ricardo Abbé, is that correct?"

Tim didn't look Ted in the eye. "Yes, sir."

"I assume you are aware that a man named Francois Benoit is serving time for the murder?"

"I am. Yes, sir."

"And you are here to tell me he didn't do it?"

"That is correct. He didn't. I did."

Ted made a sweeping gesture with his hand, as if to wipe the slate clean. "Go ahead. I'm listening."

"Sir, I shot Mr. Abbé. I did so in the belief that he had molested my sister and that I had a family obligation to take revenge."

"Did your sister urge you to kill him?"

"No, sir, my mother did."

"I want this on the record. Your mother urged you to kill Ricardo Abbé?"

"Yes, sir. She told me that he had sexually molested my sister and that I had an obligation to make him pay.

She drummed it into my head as I was growing up until it became as true as sunrise. My sister had left home for college and was estranged from my mother, so I never had a chance to ask her if what Mom had told me was true."

"Be very careful how you answer this question – you, Timothy Watkins, got on the Lechmere bus with the intention of killing the driver, Ricardo Abbé?"

"Yes, sir."

"You shot him in the head?"

"Yes, sir, that's what I did. I shot him in the head."

"Why are you stepping forward now when another man has been convicted of the crime? Remember, you are speaking on the record."

"My sister came home a week ago for the first time in years, and I had a chance to ask her if what Mom had told me was true. My sister said that Mr. Abbé was always nice to her, that he never touched her or her friends. Mom had lied to me. When that sank in, I realized what I had done. There's no excuse for it, and I'm ready to pay the price."

"Where did you get the gun?"

"Mom gave it to me. She had bought it for protection when Dad left us. I never knew my father, he left us when I was a little kid. The whole time I was growing up, I didn't know Mom had a gun."

"Where is the gun now?"

"I gave it back to Mom after I shot Mr. Abbé."

"Does your mom still have it?"

"I never asked and don't want to know."

"I'll issue a search warrant for the gun. If ballistics confirm that it was the gun used to kill Ricardo Abbé,

Francois Benoit will be a free man. For now you are free to go. Given that you came here voluntarily, I assume you will turn yourself in when I say so."

"I will. Yes, sir."

Jim spoke earnestly to Tim after they left Ted's office: "I hope someday you'll be able to weigh the good you did by confessing against the terrible thing you did and find a way to live with yourself."

Tim's eyes were focused on the far distance. At seventeen he had become an old man. "Hard to imagine that. For now I'm scared shitless of telling Mom I confessed. I'm more scared of telling her than of going to jail."

"I'll come to your arraignment and put in a good word for you, if you'd like."

"I'd like that very much. I should hate you, but I don't. Mainly I'm relieved it's over."

They shook hands and parted. Tim walked the few blocks to East Canton Street; Jim walked to The Long Gone. He felt drained of personality and soul.

A search warrant was issued for the gun. Muriel Watkins verbally resisted the search, but the gun was found in a bedroom drawer, not hidden. Apparently, Muriel Watkins had felt invulnerable. A ballistics test was done and confirmed that the gun was the weapon used to kill Ricardo Abbé.

It took a week of motions and hearings for Francois Benoit to be released from prison. A local TV station recorded his exit. When asked by the correspondent if was he grateful to be free, Benoit sneered, "Why should I be grateful? I should never have been locked up."

Tim Watkins was tried in juvenile court for second degree murder. Muriel Watkins was tried as an adult for aiding and abetting murder. Both were found guilty. Muriel's prison sentence as an adult was longer than her son's as a minor.

*

Jim unwound by spending a week with Pat in Vermont. The first snow had fallen and mornings were bitter cold. A wrong had been righted, justice had been served, etc., etc., but Jim felt horrible for everyone touched by the murder. All's well that ends well, my ass. Too many people had suffered: Ricardo Abbé and his grieving widow, Misha; the wrongly convicted Francois Benoit; and Timothy Watkins, who was both killer and victim. Muriel Watkins was the one person that Jim didn't feel sorry for.

Jim and Pat were at the dinner table the second night. The Connecticut River Valley looked subdued in the snow, as if the river had been put on hold. Jim could envision 'do not disturb' captioning the scene.

"The valley is peaceful tonight, isn't?" Jim said to Pat.

"Yes, it is. Why are you frowning? You should be smiling."

"I'm frowning?"

"Yes, you're frowning."

"I guess I'm realizing how close Benoit came to having to spend 25 years in prison."

"But he didn't, thanks to you. Good, now you're smiling."

"I'm not smiling about Benoit, I'm wondering how to spend the $100 Ted owes me. How can I spend it for maximum humiliation effect?"

"Don't rub it in, Jim. Remember, Ted's a good friend."

"Rub it in? Me? Never." Jim got up from the table.

"Where are you going?"

"To the kitchen to open a better bottle of wine. If ever a night deserved a good red, tonight's the night."

He returned with a bottle of Chateau Petrus. "This is worth more than the house."

He opened it at the table and sniffed the cork. "Oh, no!"

"What's wrong?"

Jim couldn't stop laughing. "Wouldn't you know? It's corked!"